Cover Photo: Iris Ohlinger Sipolski Mondy

TOO EARLY FOR FLOWERS: THE STORY OF A POLIO MOTHER

TOO EARLY FOR FLOWERS: THE STORY OF A POLIO MOTHER

KURT SIPOLSKI

Printed in the United States of America
ISBN: 0692636560
ISBN 9780692636565
ISBN 9781311779281
Cover Art: AquaZebra Book Cover Designs
Publisher: K-S Publications
Information: KSPublications1@aol.com
Library of Congress Control Number: 2016902851
Registered: Writer's Guild of America

ACKNOWLEDGEMENTS

Based on a true story. Optioned for a motion picture.

This portrait could not have been possible without the support from my family and friends, and those many people from around the world who contacted me after the memoir of my mother was published, prompting this novella.

Especially important were the personal stories I incorporated into this novella from polio survivors and their families: their battles, quiet dignity and great pride.

I also thank the Salk Institute, Rotary International and the World Health Organization for their encouragement in my bringing polio awareness to the public, because sadly, this disease still haunts the world many years after a vaccine.

This is written with the belief that only with the awareness and aid of First World countries will Third World countries succeed in ending polio.

But this is more than a glimpse into the lives of the unsung heroines, the world's polio mothers. It is a story of an everyday woman facing the adversities of life through faith, love, and acceptance.

—❧—

"A mother's love for her child is like nothing else in the world. It knows no law, no pity. It dares all things and crushes down remorselessly all that stands in its path."

AGATHA CHRISTIE

"Jesus chooses only the bravest boys to have polio. God will always keep His eye on you to see how you are doing. And you are so little...you have lots of adventures in front of you."

IRIS SIPOLSKI

"...And now I know that we must lift the sail
And catch the winds of destiny
Wherever they drive the boat.
To put meaning in one's life may end in madness,
But life without meaning is the torture
Of restlessness and vague desire—
It is a boat longing for the sea and yet afraid."

EDGAR LEE MASTERS

"...An opal-hearted country,
A wilful, lavish land —
All you who have not loved her,
You will not understand —
Though earth holds many splendours,
Wherever I may die,
I know to what brown country
My homing thoughts will fly."

DOROTHEA MACKELLAR

"If you are lucky enough to have lived in Paris as a young
man, then wherever you go for the rest of your life it
stays with you, for Paris is a moveable feast."

ERNEST HEMINGWAY

TABLE OF CONTENTS

FOREWORD

An Australian friend of mine once observed, "You Yanks tell everybody everything about your life. We are much more reserved. But in America you can learn about a person's whole life by sitting next to them on the bus, whether you want to listen or not."

Mom wasn't like that. She came from an era when personal things were personal things. I often asked her to sit down and write her life for me, and she said she would but she never did. I guess it was either too personal to share or too personal to relive.

So I filled in some blanks, maybe rightly or wrongly, but to me it gives some clarification and closure. You can see that I have stepped back and am observing this family and the tragedies and triumphs that passed their way.

Please, let me tell you about my mother, Iris.

ALBUM

While *Too Early for Flowers* is fiction, the story is based on real characters, although some names, times and events are changed. Following are photographs of the Sipolski family over a span of locales, decades and oceans.

Iris and Edmond Sipolski, Wedding Day, *Kewanee, Illinois,*1942

Paternal Grandmother Harriet Sipolski, Kurt, and brother Jimmy, *Lexington, Virginia*

Jim, Graduation, Virginia Military Institute, *Lexington, Virginia,* 1965

Kurt, Christmas, *Adelaide, South Australia*, 1969

Kurt, International House, *Paris, France, 1971*

‒‒‒‒‒‒‒‒‒⬦⬦⬦‒‒‒‒‒‒‒‒‒

Chapter 1

1940

Iris stood at the open train window, laughing and waving to her little family down on the platform. It was nearly dawn. Her mother, Ida, stood next to the brick station wall, a thin hanky at her nose and eyes, her winter coat pulled tightly in front of her, trying to keep the steam from the train off her legs. Iris' younger sister Muriel, also in tears, reached up and touched her hand.

"Come back soon," Muriel pleaded to her 18-year-old sister, who was magnificent in a raccoon coat, her wavy chestnut hair resting on its high shoulders.

"Muriel, I'm never coming back to Hardscrabble, Illinois," she shouted above the rumbling train. The sun lit up her face and freckled nose, and a light wind blew curls of her chestnut hair across her forehead.

"I'm going to see the world, and Washington, D.C. is my first stop!"

She knew the people nearby could hear her. She wanted everyone to know of her happiness and her success. Iris glanced past the station house to the dirty row of Negro houses, and caught the eye of a fat woman in a stretched red flannel shirt. The woman looked at Iris with a long gaze she didn't know how to interpret. It was sadness, or resignation. Could it be dislike? Iris broke off the look.

The train lurched away and their hands separated. Muriel yelled, "Iris, Iris."

Chapter 2

1949-50

"Iris, Iris." The large black hand of the porter was gently shaking her shoulder. "Wake up, Miss Iris. It's morning. You're almost in Hardscrabble."

She awoke from her dream, remembering that dawn in 1940. She glanced at the black window and saw only her reflection. She tried to nudge her two sons awake and felt like she was entering an enormous black hole, remembering that morning.

She and Ida had fought the morning she caught that train to Washington. Her mother did not want Iris to leave the security of their home to traipse all across the country. France had just fallen to the Germans and everyone talked about America entering the war. Iris had never been more than three hours away from Hardscrabble. Ida hadn't either.

"Washington might be dangerous if the President gets us into another war," Ida said.

"Mother, please. Don't ruin this day for me. I worked very hard to get that secretarial job at the Pentagon. You still have Muriel here so you won't be lonely even though Daddy's dead. But Hardscrabble is just too small for me. Golly, ugly old Neville Brand got out of our class and is an actor in Hollywood! I'm staying with some girls who seem really nice, so you shouldn't worry."

When Ida worried, she didn't talk and she wasn't talking now. Iris had to wonder if her mother was concerned about her well-being or resentful of her opportunity, but dismissed it as an evil, unkind thought.

Iris knew Washington would only be her first stop in her world travels. After a year or two, she could probably get transferred to Brussels, or maybe even Paris.

"When I have kids, I'll let them be whomever they want and go where they want," Iris vowed to herself. She hadn't realized she spoke aloud till she glanced at Ida's eyes.

Iris looked down at six-year-old Jimmy as he slept, his red hair mussed on her lap, then over at her blond-haired three-year-old Grayson lying on his back, his good leg resting on the floor, his bad leg outstretched. Her mind half-numb from the events of last week, Iris was desperate to get off the train. She had studied her boys on the train ride, looked out at the gray and barren states, and studied them again. She knew what she had to do.

"I'll get the little one, Miss Iris," said Ben, the porter. "Yes, just don't put any pressure on Grayson's polio leg," she cautioned, and watched Ben as he carefully followed her instructions.

At that moment she looked up to see the head porter at the doorway, scowling, his hands on his hips. "Ben, you uppity nigger!" His black features were incredulous. "What you mean by calling a white lady by her Christian name?" Ben, a giant, stared humbly at the floor of the cabin.

Iris stood to her full height, barely reaching the head porter's chest. She smoothed the front of her rumpled suit. "My name is Mrs. Sipolski. When people try to say it, it sounds like 'Miss Upholstery.' And Ben has helped me with little

Grayson all the way from Virginia." She turned her back to him. "Yes…m…Mrs… ppil …" the head porter's voice trailed away.

Impulsively, Iris giggled as Ben looked away in respect for his superior.

For a second, Ben studied her hazel eyes. He wanted to describe Miss Iris to his wife when he returned home. Iris was a great beauty. Not, perhaps, like a Greer Garson but a Theresa Wright. The kind of beauty that mostly came from within, the kind of beauty that did not threaten men nor women, but that both sexes admired.

She could see the sign approaching. Hardscrabble, Illinois. Pop 16,000. "Sixteen thousand and three," she thought.

Grayson raised his head from Ben's shoulder and giggled at his face. "Are you my daddy?"

"Now, Gray," Iris said, "don't be silly. You know your daddy is in heaven."

Gray rested his head against the man's wide shoulder and promptly fell asleep, just as the sun pierced Hardscrabble.

Ben lifted Gray high up, careful to not poke the full leg brace sideways, clearing a path down the aisle to the door as Muriel and her husband Brad waited on the platform below.

Iris grimaced and her eyes shut tight to hold back the conflicting emotions of the meeting: The pain of death, the warmth of family, the end of her journey. There was time enough for that later.

The looks on the train were no different from the other looks of the past year. If there were children, they stared at Gray's brace poking out the bottom of his pants. The men would smile softly and nod at her with sympathy and understanding. The women would look directly into her eyes in sadness and blame at her tragedy, and hope there was something different about her than them, that there was something wrong with Iris, that she had been careless, that they would be a better mother; that their own children would be safe. Polio could be anywhere and a good mother should know that.

Only a week before, Iris and the boys had gone shopping, and as they approached a mother and her little girl, the woman took out her handkerchief and held it against the girl's nose and mouth as Gray passed. He looked at the girl, up at Iris, and back at the girl but said nothing.

The stares reminded Iris of the one her mother had given her long ago after she forgot to look after their terrier, Corky.

Corky had run into the street and was killed under the wheels of a tractor. It read, "You only had one job to do and look what happened."

Iris could not hold their gaze.

Iris wasn't angered or insulted by this. She honestly didn't know if she would act any differently from those women if Gray hadn't caught the virus, and she was facing some other little boy or girl. Illness was humbling, enlightening.

"Ma'am, will little Gray ever be normal? Polio's an awful thing." Ben's brown and gentle eyes moved Iris deeply.

She hesitated, thinking of meeting President Roosevelt. He was in his wheelchair when he came into the war office at the Pentagon where she worked before she met her husband, Bunny.

"God knows." It wasn't an exclamation. It was a prayer. She hadn't noticed that Gray awoke and heard Ben's words. She opened her black clutch purse.

"Ben, take this." Iris handed him a five dollar bill, and then another. "Why, ma'am, can you afford this?" Ben said. Immediately, he regretted saying it.

"I wish it could be more. Thank you, Ben." Her tiny hand was able only to squeeze the side of his hand. Her open face had the innocence of a schoolgirl.

"You are a great lady," Ben said.

The black, freezing air bolted Iris back; she was so used to the over-heated, smoky train. She stepped down.

As she walked to their car, Iris glanced back. "Some of those darkies can be so nice," she thought.

Ben was watching her thinking, "Some of those whities can be so nice."

The women embraced for several moments, and then Iris said hello to Brad. Muriel was still shy around her big sister and waited for her to speak first after they settled in the car, Iris and the boys in back, the three small suitcases in the trunk of the DeSoto.

"Those Japs," Iris said. "They've ruined my life. Bunny goes off to war right after our wedding and I see him twice in four years." She looked down at Gray and Jimmy. "The war's over, Bunny comes home with headaches and dies at 28."

"I know, Iris, we're all so, so sorry about Bunny." Muriel had read and re-read the telegram and remembered every word of the short telephone conversation saying Bunny had died.

As the car drove the short distance to Ida's, Iris looked outside at the neat little houses, their lights just coming on. Families were preparing breakfast. Mothers and fathers and children were in those houses.

Anger had been her fury, her friend, and her fuel. It had been her focus where one was impossible to fix on before. It had served its purpose.

There, it was off her chest. It was said and it was over. Bitterness had to be replaced by being a single mother. She had to find a job. And she had to learn to live with her mother again.

Jimmy, like any six-year-old, talked on and on of the train trip and the people they saw and the food they ate. Gray rubbed at his braced leg with both hands but didn't say anything. He stopped when he saw Iris glance at him, and he looked out the window.

The dam broke. The two daughters burst into tears once Ida appeared at the door, wiping her hands on that constant, faded blue apron. Reunions should not be like this.

Ida hadn't changed, really. She looked old when Iris left and she looked old now, wisps of gray hair poking out of her hairnet. Iris had visited twice, each time with a new baby boy. Maybe Ida's face was a bit thinner. She was even tinier than Iris.

They all talked at once, sometimes to each other, sometimes in a whisper, like when Muriel asked Gray if he wanted the leather straps loosened a bit. He looked at his mother before shaking his head "no."

By the time Brad had the suitcases unloaded, the women's tears had turned to laughter as all three enjoyed the sleepy little boys, curious at their new home and yard. It was far different from their stone farmhouse near Alexandria, Virginia with its wide stretches of pasture, the running white fence, the mares nuzzling their colts, the hazy Blue Mountains in the distance.

Smoky bacon smells were in the air, the grease still in the iron skillet waiting for sunny side eggs and homemade bread.

This tidy little house had always been in the family. Covered in brown tarpaper, it had a wide wooden porch that Ida would scrub with a bucket of soapy water and a broom all through the warmer weather. Two thick, round wooden columns on either side of the three concrete stairs somehow made the little house look important. She always insisted it be kept immaculate inside and out.

The front door opened to a large dining room, unused except for Thanksgiving and Christmas. There were two bedrooms off the living room where the piano sat. The "bathroom" off the kitchen had neither a shower nor a bath, but just a toilet, a musty closet and a Singer sewing machine. It would be back to sponge baths for Iris, with water heated on the stove because there was no hot water heater. But now she had two little boys to bathe in the kitchen sink.

For some reason the kitchen was unusually large. Off to one side, a six-inch rubber strap poked out of the floor. It was nailed to the trap door, which opened to the old cellar with its dirt smell, rough white limestone walls, and jars and jars of canned fruit and vegetables.

The furnace was there. Twice a month the coal truck would pull next to the house and dump its black load through the cellar window, to be fed into the furnace, heavy shovel by heavy shovel through the winter months.

Iris walked back to Ida's bedroom, sat on the bed opposite her mother's, and slowly took off her hat, her gloves, her shoes and her black suit. She removed her stockings and rubbed each foot. She had worn the same clothes since Bunny's burial at Arlington National Cemetery, not even changing for the train.

She slipped on a turquoise sweater and tan slacks and bent forward to brush her thick hair. She couldn't remember anything in her whole life being so refreshing, and brushed several more times.

That night she would burn the pile of funeral clothes as she stoked the furnace in the cellar. Iris barely looked in the hall mirror as she rejoined her mother. Muriel and Brad had left by then, anxious to get back to their kids and relieve their neighbor.

The comfort of her childhood home and kitchen smells relaxed everyone. Later, Ida, Iris, and Jimmy walked around the yard, after Iris sat Gray in a chair near the window so he could watch them. She propped up his bad leg on another chair, gathered her scarf and jacket and went outside. Every few minutes Iris would turn and wave at him and he would wave back. Gray traced the edges of the glass against the pane. He was becoming used to being removed from people and had already accepted it as normal.

Suddenly, Iris bent down and scooped back a bit of snow, existing only because it lay in the shadow of the house. It had tinges of gray from the sooty coal smoke. She looked at the shoots sprouting on that remarkably warm March morning which soon would be heavy pink peonies. It was too early for flowers, but she saw the shoots all around her…the bent and dead-looking old-fashioned white roses would be so heavy with perfume in the summer they would be abuzz with bumblebees. The brown Queen Anne's Lace, taller than she was, would be frosty white. Irises of all colors. The pussy willows, the lilies of the valley, the purple, heavily perfumed lilacs…they were all to come. Year after year Ida would have the girls take out the vegetable cuttings, eggshells and coffee grounds and put them on the flowerbeds. Decades of rich loam had enriched the plants.

There was peace now, and there was promise.

It was early evening when they had settled in, Gray and Jimmy in the double bed in one bedroom, and Iris and Ida in the other. Before going to her room, Iris sat on the boys' bed.

"You know, things are going to be different now that your dad is in heaven." She hoped the boys would say something, anything, to guide Iris in her talk. But they sat, their backs against the headboard, waiting for her to continue.

"Well, we all have nice memories of the farm and the animals and our life there, and we always have to keep those things in our mind, but we have a new life now so we really can't dwell on those past things too much.

"Jimmy's going to a new school so he'll have new friends and I know we'll all be happy with your Gram."

Jimmy asked, "Will Gray get a new leg doctor?"

Iris' throat thickened suddenly and she tried to speak in the same tone.

"Yes, honey, maybe not in this town but a bigger town, and we'll all make sure he'll get better."

Iris thought she spoke convincingly.

Jimmy spoke again. "Mom, can you sing us one of those war songs like you used to?"

The boys slid under the covers, the blanket under their chins.

"How about 'Someone to Watch Over Me?'"

There's a somebody I'm longin' to see
I hope that he, turns out to be
Someone who'll watch over me

I'm a little lamb who's lost in the wood
I know I could, always be good
To one who'll watch over me

Although he may not be the man some
Girls think of as handsome
To my heart he carries the key

Won't you tell him please to put on some speed
Follow my lead, oh, how I need
Someone to watch over me

She paused. Jimmy had his eyes closed.

Gray was frowning at her. "Too sad, Mom."

Iris smiled on the way back to her bedroom. Gray's personality had changed so much since he left the hospital and had to cope with the leg brace. He was so bright and exuberant before, and now could be introspective and distant. There was work ahead for her.

She stopped at the bay window in the living room. A lone streetlight vainly attempted to cut through the darkness. She pulled back the white lace curtain and looked out.

Iris continued to reflect: "*Then, just as things were starting to settle down again, Bunny dies. Just like that. Gone.*" Iris moved the curtain to her nose. It had the same smell of "old" she remembered as a little girl. Only last week she had her own home and it smelled of oak burning in the fireplace, and cinnamon, and fresh, crisp air when Bunny would stomp in, shaking the snow off his boots. She took a deep breath and walked in the dark to her bedroom.

There were no sounds of contented sleep. Iris pulled off her sweater in the silent room. "Mother, I know you're awake. When you're upset you don't talk, and we have to talk."

Silence. Then Ida spoke, "You come home twice in all these years to show me the boys, like you couldn't wait to leave here, and now you come back."

"Mother, when I left here after high school I was determined to show you I could make it on my own. And I did. But I thought of you and missed you every day." She moved to Ida's bed and sat down. She looked down at her hands in her lap and twisted the gold ring. "OK, I was pretty stuck on myself. But I got taught a good lesson, and I just need you now more than any time in my life.

"You have to love me like a daughter and love me as an adult. You are a widow with kids and now I'm a widow with kids. It's not going to be easy with the boys. I just don't know how to raise Gray the right way and I need your advice. But at the same time I have to feel I am in charge with the boys. Oh, I don't know, I guess it's complicated."

She thought she heard Ida sniffle.

"And there are some things you should know about last week, Mother. Things that have to stay just between you and me."

She and Ida talked for an hour, and Iris told her the many and private details of Bunny's death, the burial, her urge to get home. Iris went to her bed and slipped under the wool blankets. Her mother asked something, but didn't get an answer. Too tired to think of the past or the present or the future, Iris had fallen deeply asleep.

When she awoke and walked into the kitchen, Gray was eating Cheerios with his grandmother, his father's sepia-toned photograph propped up between them. His crutches were leaned against the icebox.

"Thanks, Mother. I was exhausted," Iris said. She kissed the top of his head and rested her hand on Gray's blond hair as she looked outside at Jimmy hunting wild Indians with an old broomstick rifle. She had to get some toys for the boys.

Later, washing dishes with water heated on the stove, the two talked about money, or really, the lack of it. Since Bunny had died after the war, there were no death benefits. His life insurance was still in his mother's name so that was gone.

Fortunately, the March of Dimes paid all Gray's bills for the therapy, visits, and braces. She knew there would be expensive operations to come, too, and they would all be taken care of. Iris didn't consider this charity, but merely good people helping good people and when her chance came she would do the same.

Bunny's parents had kept the farm since it was in their name only, so she couldn't count on any income there. The parting gifts to her were three one-way tickets to Illinois. It was something she accepted and did not want to rationalize.

The canning factory where Ida worked was closed for the winter season so the women had a bit of unemployment insurance.

Iris studied the want ads. That afternoon she dressed carefully in a dark blue suit and white faux pearl earrings. She was glad she hadn't burned the black gloves. She wore low heels because she had to make the rounds, hunting for secretarial work at an attorney's office, and the Montgomery Wards, and an insurance firm.

—∞∞∞—

Iris accepted the job at the insurance company and would begin the next morning. It was a small office, just her and four men. She could look out on Main Street from her desk to the park with its newly installed War Memorial. She would see it every day.

A car wasn't even a remote consideration. She would walk to and from their home.

Word swiftly got around that Iris had returned. One of her high school friends eyed Iris from the drug store as she passed, saying to her boyfriend, "And this is the girl who said she was never coming back to town? That this town wasn't good enough for her? Just like Bette Davis!"

The boy replied, "Well, she got further than you and I probably will," and sipped his Coke. "And her poor little kid..."

"Well, I just hope no one gets polio from him," she added. The boy stared at her and wondered why he even liked her.

The days and weeks began to roll into one another as a routine developed in the little tarpaper house.

Jimmy entered first grade, just a block from their home. Ida stayed with Gray during the day. Iris walked to work, then home for lunch, and then helped her mother with the dinner after work.

After the dishes were done, Iris would lay an oilcloth on the kitchen table in preparation for Gray's leg exercises. It was important that the muscles didn't cramp and tighten up since the leg was basically immobile.

Gray would lie on his stomach in his underwear as Iris bent his bad leg. "Hold, hold," she would say as Gray tried and tried to keep her from pulling the leg back down. "Good, honey," she said even though Gray could barely offer any resistance. Then he would lie on his good side while she pulled his bad leg up, scissor-fashion and helped him raise and lower it. Then he would sit on the side of the table and she would try to get him to extend the leg. He braced himself with his hands, leaning back, straining to move any muscle in the leg. Sometimes Iris thought it moved.

"Ow, Mom. Gee, that hurts," Gray cried out as the tight muscles refused to stretch. "Mom, you're hurting me!"

"Yes, I know. So let's get it over and done with," Iris said, trying to sound upbeat.

"I don't like you when you do this, Mom."

Frustrated, Iris snapped, "Well, I'm going to help you but first I have to hurt you." She remembered the Australian polio pioneer Sister Kenny had said that and Iris knew the scene would be repeated for years to come.

One evening Gray asked, "Mom, how did I get polio? Jimmy said I used to eat flies for breakfast."

"Well, Jimmy is a little smarty-pants 'cause no one knows how people get polio. You might have met someone who had it, or eaten something. But it's called a virus and goes into your brain I think, and then down your backbone.

And you know, honey, lots and lots of little kids can't walk nearly as well as you, and some can't walk at all."

"But why do kids get it?" Gray asked.

"Oh, I guess because their bodies aren't't strong enough. But you know, Gray, I met President Roosevelt once, and he was in a wheel chair from it. So you are better off than the president was."

They both were quiet then, aside from groans whenever Iris stretched his leg or Gray tried in vain to comply with her instructions.

Sometimes they would talk about their day, do the alphabet. Sometimes, rarely, she talked of the farm in Virginia but she would just as soon leave that in the past.

"Mom, remember when you were on one horse and Daddy and Jimmy and me were on the other and we stopped at that stream and that big snake came at you?" Gray asked.

"Oh, yes, honey, that big, old, ugly Copperhead."

"And then daddy made his horse stomp it? And Jimmy was laughing so hard that Daddy had to pound him on the back 'cause he started coughing?"

"Yes, I think he was scared and excited at the same time," Iris said.

"Does Jimmy get scared?" he asked.

"Oh, honey, everyone gets scared," Iris said, dreading the question that would come up next.

"What has scared you the most in all your whole life, Mom?" Gray asked.

She knew the answer as well as she knew her own heart or Gray's name.

She put her forehead next to his and stared in his eyes until they both were cross-eyed. Gray always squealed because they both looked so funny.

"You know, I think you ask more questions that any little boy in town."

Then Gray asked another. "Mom, didn't dad and granddad fight a lot? I think I remember that."

"You remember that? Hmmm. Now, turn on your side and let's do the consonants," Iris said, changing the subject.

Sometimes Jimmy would watch from the doorway, frowning, his arms crossed in front of himself. He stared, but said nothing.

Iris was nearly as tired as Gray by the time they had finished, and bed was welcome. Her arms and back were as weary as her mind.

She would play bridge with "the girls" once every two weeks and catch up on the town gossip. Iris would draw the line, though, if it ever became mean or catty. Maybe at another time in her life she would have joined in, but not now. She wasn't sure she completely liked the disposition of women.

Sometimes she and Muriel would go to a movie. Iris was not discontented.

Overall, it was a remarkably smooth transition as the months passed, and in general Ida respected the fact that her daughter was a grown woman with whom she shared widowhood experiences, so she did not treat her like a girl.

Ida was more tolerant raising the boys than she had been raising the girls. Maybe it was her age or just a different way she had of dealing with boys, but she allowed them more freedom, and usually let them settle their own fights until they reached a certain crescendo.

Iris remembered how strict she had been, controlling everything that happened in their house, even waiting on the front steps when her father came home with his paycheck. His Irish blood told him that paychecks had to be spent at the tavern, and woe to him if he did that. Iris really thought that her moving back had given her mother another, happier chance at life. Most importantly, Gray did not always need his crutches. Iris dared hope he would be normal.

At dinner one evening, Gray spoke.

"I had a good day today. I walked down to the railroad tracks in back of the school to wave at the people on the train when they went past. Some of them waved back. One man who looked like Dad waved at me and smiled."

Iris shot a look at Jimmy as he opened his mouth. He closed his mouth.

"It's fun to see people going someplace, but kind of sad when the train is gone and you can't even hear it anymore, Gray said.

"Yes," Iris said. She was realizing Gray was developing rapidly at analyzing ordinary, everyday things. She also was concerned at his independence, that he could just take off whenever he felt like it, but decided for the moment to leave it alone.

"Mom, I saw a policeman on the way back. He even had a gun. I want to be a policeman when I grow up."

The women averted their eyes and remained silent, scraping their forks across the half-empty plates, pretending to search for another morsel, avoiding Gray's innocent words.

"You'll never be a cop. Who would hire you? You can't run or jump over a fence. You'd never catch a bad guy. You'll never be in the army like dad and granddad and me."

With that, Gray scooted his chair back, walked the few steps to Jimmy, and kicked him in the shin with his leg brace. He collapsed to the floor and howled as Gray calmly sat back at the table.

"Ow, Mom, Gray kicked me right on my bone...ow...ow...ow...it hurts, Mom."

Iris took a mouthful of mashed potatoes and turned to Jimmy, chewing. She had figured rightly that it was more sound than fury. She swallowed. "Are you bleeding?"

Jimmy pulled up the pant leg and looked and looked, moving the leg from side to side.

"Not on the outside, but probably inside my bone I am," he screamed.

There was silence. Everyone else continued to eat.

"Isn't anyone going to say anything?" he asked.

It was Ida's turn. "I'd say you were lucky Gray doesn't have braces on both legs!"

So unexpected was the outburst from this little woman Iris laughed so hard she spat out her food. Jimmy was speechless and then he started laughing. Gray had no idea what everyone was laughing at but he laughed, too.

Evenings were spent quietly, playing a board game like Ropes & Ladders, sometimes just listening to the radio while Iris caught up on her mending. If a song came on like "How Much is That Doggy in the Window" they all sang along with it, and Gray got to do his favorite part, woof like the dog.

Often, Ida would stretch Gray out on the davenport and massage his bad leg.

One time, he said, "Gram, do you wish I was normal?"

She and Iris were so taken they couldn't think of what to say. Iris concentrated on the sock and sewing kit in her lap.

"I mean, if the exercises and rubbing don't work, and I will always be like this, will that disappoint you or Mom?"

Ida looked at Iris. It was a terrible question for her, and she didn't know how to respond.

Iris desperately wanted to throw down her sewing kit, kneel next to him, hold his hand and put her cheek next to his, but knew it would give too much gravity to the subject. Instead, she tried to be casual.

"Oh, honey, of course we wouldn't be disappointed. Just like when Jimmy swings at a ball, we hope for the best, but if he doesn't hit it, that's still okay."

She knew she wasn't exactly answering Gray's question. Because she knew she *would* be disappointed. She couldn't imagine Gray as a man of 40 dragging that heavy brace around. She couldn't stand to think of it. What a life.

A bright bubble of blood blossomed from the needle prick.

Chapter 3

1951

Why had she been so anxious to get out of Hardscrabble? Why had she felt she was entering a black hole when her train had pulled into the station? She had her girlfriends from grade school and high school, she liked the insurance company although the name had conveyed some foreboding (Grimm Insurance) she had her best friend, her sister Muriel. When Iris left Hardscrabble, Muriel was just a teenager, and now she was a woman with two sons of her own. The sisters had their hair cut and styled the same way. They sometimes looked like twins.

At least once a week the two would meet downtown for egg salad sandwiches and black coffee. Iris was more honest with her than perhaps anyone in her life, except Bunny.

She shared confidences about Gray.

"You know, Gray was taken from me right away when he got polio. I pleaded with them that I would take the chance of getting polio myself, that I HAD to be with him, but they put him in isolation...can you imagine? *Can you imagine?* A little sick boy, can't even be held by his mother? Suddenly surrounded by

strangers with masks? I can't imagine. He must have thought he had done something wrong. I didn't even have time to tell him or explain. I have to wonder
how that may affect him later.

"Oh, that first time was so hard. Gray held out his little arms to us to come
and get him, but of course, we couldn't. I mean, no one knew that much about
the disease. We had to go outside and wave to him from the window below
when the nurses held him up…

"And he cried and cried up there and I was just about to myself when…
hahaha …Jimmy…hahaha …pulled up his shirt and waved his hands in the air
and did the hula hoochy-koochy. Wiggling his little hips back and forth and just
being so silly. Oh, and then Gray was screaming but this time he was laughing…
and, of course, Bunny and I were bent over howling. Oh, Jimmy was a big help,
and he showed us the way."

Muriel laughed, and enjoyed her memory.

"You know this, Muriel, I'm not telling you anything. But family is THE most important thing in the world. I sure learned that lesson. Me and all my big travel plans.

"I don't know how much to encourage Gray now. There are no books or
role models. I can't suggest impossible standards like his becoming President
like Roosevelt. I mean, he was a grown man when he got polio. He was wealthy
and had every resource. I did tell him that I bet when he grew up he would meet
the President like I did.

"I talk to Gray about traveling the world if he loses his braces, going to
Europe…Africa…the South Pacific like I wanted to before I met Bunny, but
even that seems like an impossible dream.

"But those leg exercises are so tedious…I have to distract him. I went on and
on about Australia the other night. You know, Bunny went to Darwin after the
Japs bombed it…he said Australia is like an open canvas…a person can reinvent
himself down there. Gray does like those stories."

They sat in silence, then breaking the grimness with talk of how hard it was
to get stylish dresses when you are only five feet tall and don't want to look like
a 13-year-old.

As much as Iris had loved D.C., the friends she met had come there from
all over the U.S. to work, and there had not been that sense of history and

familiarity she found with her sister and their friends. And there was a certain feeling she got at the Pentagon she didn't like. The departments didn't seem to co-operate much, and ultimately all the employees got involved in the jealousies.

One of her roommates from DC, with the crazy nickname of Crummee, was about to marry a Senator. But reminiscing about Iris' past was lost with her friends from Hardscrabble. She became adept at learning from the past and not living in it.

At times she would look at Muriel across the lunch counter at Woolworth's, and Iris wondered if she knew how lucky she was--having a cute home, a loving husband, and two healthy kids. Iris was happy for her, maybe even envious. She was getting tired of sponge baths, no hot water, of the ever present financial concern. But she would not marry again nor hope for an easier future. Her life was her two sons now.

A woman--no matter how attractive, with two kids, especially with one disabled, was not much bait for any bachelor. Iris shrugged it off.

This was a life she had settled into completely.

She liked the walks to and from work. There were so many big, shady oak trees along the way. It gave her a chance to think, away from home and work.

One time, on her walk home, she was thinking of the previous night. Her mother had talked about the trees in their own front yard, two huge maples and one tall old hickory tree.

"The nerve of that person," Ida had said at dinner, talking about the man who had knocked on her door earlier. "He wanted to give me $90 to cut down that hickory tree to sell it for firewood. Imagine that. That beautiful old tree to be cut down and burnt?"

Jimmy asked, "Is $90 a lot of money?"

"Yes, it's a whole lot of money," his grandmother said. "But some things you just can't take money for. What kind of a world would it be if you just sold off and destroyed beautiful things for the money? It's like selling a part of your soul. I wouldn't want to be part of it."

Iris had to agree, but that $90 could have gone a long way.

As Iris walked on, she studied the old brick sidewalk set in that herring-bone-style that ran all through the town. The brick factory certainly was a big business, one of the town's mainstays. That and the canning factory, the big glass plant, Owen's. It was a pretty solid town.

There was always someone she knew along the route:

"Hi, Iris, how's little Gray?" they would say, or something similar. Now and again women would be offended as Iris merely smiled and walked on. It was because the sisters looked so much alike now, that people often mistook one for the other. After a while, the sisters would smile brightly at everyone for fear of offending anyone. They were known as two of the friendliest women in town!

One time returning home she was interrupted in her thoughts. Jimmy came running up, wearing a headband with a pheasant feather poking out the back. Brad had shot two pheasants that fall and divided up the tail feathers between his boys and hers. Iris recognized the headband as the elastic waist of his new underpants, and the war paint as her favorite lipstick, but just didn't want to get into that now.

He was bare-chested and brown as a berry from the sun.

"Mom, I don't like playing cowboys and Indians with Gray," he said.

"Oh good," Iris thought. *"At last a simple problem."*

"Why not, honey?"

"'Cause he's a cowboy and I shot him and he won't fall down. He doesn't play right."

"Well, think about this for a minute." She reached down and held his hand as they walked towards the house. "If he falls down he has to get back up again, doesn't he? And you know how hard that is for him."

"Oh," Jimmy said. "Well, why didn't he just tell me?"

"Sometimes everything can't be explained for one reason or another. In life you have to kind of look at all sides of things to understand people. That's the difference in somebody being smart and being wise."

Jimmy pulled his hand away from hers. He ran toward Gray.

"Bet you can't shoot me, Gray."

BAM! Jimmy pirouetted over and over again, agonizingly, shot through the heart by Wild Bill Hickok. He fell to the ground and laid there, spread-eagled. He was as dead as a doornail. Then one eye opened, a tiny slit, to see if his mother had been watching. She had.

Iris laughed. "What a little ham I have."

Jimmy raised his head. "Well, this little ham wants a little cookie!"

"Me, too, Mom," Gray said. He reached up for the wooden column to support him as he struggled up the concrete steps.

"Here Gray, let me help," Jimmy said and grabbed him by the arm.

Iris flushed and felt a lump rise in her throat as she followed the two boys into the kitchen. She knew something important had just happened to all three of them.

Muriel and Iris loved their lunches together. Sometimes they talked about their older sister, Leola, and her family and her work at the Westclox factory in nearby Ottawa. Painting radium dials was highly skilled and highly paid. Leola had a great sense of style and often would buy Iris a blouse or purse or pure silk scarf (not just nylon) and Iris loved her thoughtfulness.

Leola had spoken of her panic when the telegram arrived telling her of Gray and his polio. "Gray has polio. Left side OK." She had run out of the house, grabbing Sharon, Ron, and Johnnie and pulling them into the house.

"Little Gray has polio! Polio! My Lord! Polio in that little out-of-the-way place. So it can happen here! You kids stay inside."

They all groaned and argued but Leola was firm, at least for the rest of the day. The later cacophony showed her that she would get sick with three kids penned up on a sunny day.

Later that night she confided to her husband Frank, "My Lord, what if little Gray doesn't make it?" Then she paused. "But what if he does? Will he be all twisted up? In an iron lung?" The more she talked, the worse the consequences became.

Frank didn't say much. "Those are healthy kids. He'll pull through, just you wait and see."

Leola had heard that cotton balls soaked in rubbing alcohol pinned on the window screen would attract and hold the virus, and soon, all her windows had two cotton balls dribbling down. Years later, she was able to laugh, "Well, hell! Maybe it worked!"

Muriel drove Iris and Gray to his monthly doctor appointments in Peoria, about 60 miles away. It was a big city to them, and they loved the hustle of the big Penny's and lingered at the cosmetic counter and the notions department. Every now and then Iris would buy herself a pretty hanky, admiring it on their way home, smoothing the folds out on her knee.

Jimmy hated to go with them to the orthopedic doctor, though, and would tear out of the house running so Iris would have to leave him with her mother. The boys were becoming very independent and hard to manage. Gray would cry and stiffen up when she tried to put his brace on each morning. Once she had tried to spank him but the heavy steel belt around his waist caught the full impact of her swat and her hand stung the rest of the day.

Gray liked the old doctor. He was sympathetic, but he was firm about wearing the brace at all times. He would trace Gray's spine all the way down into his underpants to make sure it was straight. He would have Gray walk down the hall and back at least twice. It was the only time Gray would see other polio children and he didn't like it. He didn't want to think he looked like them.

One day after an appointment, Iris sat with Gray on the floor of the bathroom. He was crying. It was a humid, July morning and she was dressing him. "Mom, why did I have to get polio? Why couldn't I have just died?"

She tied the orthopedic shoe, strapped the leather calf strap, the two buckles of the leather knee pad, the leather thigh strap and buckled the leather-covered steel belt and tugged his jeans over the shoe and the brace. She knew the brace cut into his waist.

Then she stopped.

She took his hands in hers.

"But, Gray, Jesus chooses only the bravest boys. He chose you above all the little boys in town."

Gray bit into his lower lip and stifled his tears. "Am I brave?"

"Of course you are, honey. And you know that God will always keep his eye on you to see how you are doing. And you are so little...you have lots of adventures in front of you.

"Now you go outside and play with Jimmy. I have some sewing to do."

Gray looked up at the Singer sewing machine covered over with a table-cloth. "And close the door," she said.

She pressed her hanky to Gray's face and watched him walk slowly, carefully down the old gray wooden steps. He grabbed the railing with both hands, and then inched down slowly till he reached the grass.

Iris looked briefly at the crucifix above the sewing machine and burst into tears herself.

"My God, he's only a little boy! A little boy! Why did You have to do that? He has pain every day of his life. What kind of job could he ever get? Will he ever get married? How could he possibly support a family? What kind of life will he have?"

Iris glanced out the window, and then turned back to the crucifix.

"You died for our sins. So why did You die if we are still suffering from those sins? And what sin could that sweet little boy have committed to punish him his whole life?" She paused.

"Or have I sinned, and You are punishing me through little Gray? Is that what's going on?"

Then she spoke calmly, "Jesus, if I have sinned...if I was ever proud or arrogant or unkind You take it out on me. You leave my two kids alone!"

She waited for any kind of sign.

Gray looked up from the yard, saw his mother at the window, smiled and waved. But she was looking at something in the sky. A cloud or something.

Chapter 4

———⚮———

1953

I t was egg salad time, and now Muriel did the talking.
"Iris, you're almost 35. It's time to think about getting married and having a father for the boys."

Iris thought back to the man that she had met at the office a month earlier. He was tall, and very handsome. He had impossibly wavy blond hair, even with it cut short. He seemed nice and it felt good to talk to him. He offered her a ride home after work and she invited him in for coffee. His thin smile showed he had expected that, and Iris immediately became wary.

"He is an oaf," Iris thought after spending 10 minutes with him. Just too confident. His legs were spread wide apart, a smirk on his face she did not like at all. He held his unlit cigar below waist level and scratched the inside of his leg. She knew what he was implying but pretended not to notice.

"So. Your boys play sports?"

"Jimmy does. Gray doesn't." She didn't want him to know anything more about her or her family.

"A boy not play sports? Is he a fairy?"

Iris nearly fell of her chair at his crudeness.

Just then Gray came to the door, hesitated, and without his eyes leaving the man's, walked towards Iris. The man couldn't take his eyes off the brace. Iris pulled Gray up onto her lap. Without breaking a glance at the man, she said, "This man wants to know something about you, Gray."

"Oh. I didn't know he wasn't a normal boy," he stammered.

Iris said simply, "Thank you for the ride home. Goodbye."

With that he stood up, grabbed his hat off the kitchen table and walked out the door. He knew he would not be welcome there again.

It only confirmed what Iris thought about all of the men in Hardscrabble.

———

Iris took a long drag on her Camel cigarette, and let the smoke drift out.

"First of all, everyone I've met in town is either married or undesirable. And what kind of catch would I be? A woman my age with two kids? And Gray the way he is? And there's something I have to tell you."

She crushed out the cigarette.

"In Virginia, that last Thanksgiving Bunny and I had a lot of people over for dinner. We all ate too much and drank too much. We had whiskey sours before dinner and champagne and wine with dinner. All the hoity-toity crème-de-la crème from the valley were there. I really thought I had arrived. The house was smoky from the cigarettes and closed in because it was so cold out. Anyway, Gray came down with the flu that night. Well, he was sick and so cranky it wore me out. I...I...told him to hush and be a big boy.

"I asked Bunny to take me out to see 'Mildred Pierce' after. Their grandparents babysat. I was all dressed up, we had a wonderful time and I thought I had made it into society.

"The next day when I tried to get Gray out of bed he couldn't stand up. He wasn't in pain then, but was very hot. I would pull him up and he fell down like a little rag doll! He thought it was so funny. I had a terrible feeling he had polio. Of course, it was. I was just stunned. My God! It was winter! Nobody got polio in winter!"

She paused for a long time. "They closed down the theater and cleaned it for three days."

Muriel did not take her eyes off Iris. A waitress approached with a pot of coffee, surmised the mood, and turned back.

"You know," Iris continued, "Mildred Pierce was an ambitious woman who wanted to go out on a date, so they were out all evening, and when she got home she found out her little girl had come down with pneumonia. She died in the movie. Well, that's how I felt when I was with Gray during his rehabilitation in the hospital. Maybe if I was with him instead of out with Bunny he wouldn't have gotten so sick.

"I just think if I hadn't had all those people over and if we had stayed home he wouldn't have polio. I owe him my complete attention.

"Those next few days...I don't know...they were like out of some terrible nightmare...no one came over...suddenly, there were spotty cases of polio all over the place. One time I came to the polio ward...there was this woman...her name was Mrs. Armour...not that we would know each other but her picture was always in the society column...very well-to-do...she was standing next to this gurney in the hallway. She was just in her nightdress... this elegant woman...her hair was all lopsided. And her little girl was on this gurney.

"And she was dead. She looked like a little porcelain doll with her blond hair all spread out on the pillow. And Mrs. Armour had covered her up to her chin with her mink coat like she was trying to keep her warm.

"Anyway, she'd had her head in her hands and when she looked up at me she had these four little crescent cuts about each eyebrow. She hadn't realized she had dug her nails into her skin!

"She looked at me like a scared animal.

"She said that Marie was only nine, that she became ill at her birthday party.

"I remember her tugging at the fur, looking at it.

"She said, 'What does anything matter without Marie? If only she had been crippled. We could have taken care of her her whole life and loved her every minute. But she's gone. Like God just flicked off a switch.'

"Then she asked if I had child there, and I said 'Yes, a boy, but that he was going to live.' And saying that I suddenly realized I was lucky. She asked what

Gray's name was and how old he was, and I said 'two,' and she said, 'There is no greater burden than being a mother.'

"And you know, Muriel…I was even a little jealous this morning…talking about luck and stuff…in Look magazine there was a story about this Jackie Bouvier marrying a senator…Kennedy, I think…you should have seen her gown! And I thought some people just seem to have everything…beauty…money…power…she will never have to want for a thing. Her life is charmed. She and her kids will have everything."

Muriel grimaced and quickly sat forward.

"Iris, every mother blames herself when her kids get sick, and that is natural…a part of being a mother. But remember that President Roosevelt was a grown man when he got sick. Maybe you're just afraid to date again. You need a husband to take care of you, and the boys need a father."

She had a wry smile. "And we don't want you turning out like the other widow we know, raising kids on her own."

The reference to their mother was not lost on Iris, and it gave her pause.

Iris considered this for a long moment, then laughed. "Well, tomorrow I'm buying a used car. I'll get married the day after tomorrow."

The car wouldn't start. It was a big, heavy, gray Plymouth, a few years old, with not a scratch on it. And it was all hers. She was so proud of herself.

With great ceremony she sat the boys in the back and settled her suspicious mother in the front. She was going to show Ida that she had a good business sense. Iris turned the key in the ignition and only got a faint clickclickclick.

"Oh, it's nothing," she said, doubting the words, convinced by Ida's look that she had made a big $300 mistake.

Flustered, Iris hurried inside and pulled out the phone book. The rest got out of the car and sat on the stoop steps.

Nothing under "A." Under "B" was "Bill's Garage." Then she waited for the party line to clear. For some reason, the man who answered knew where the house was, and said he would be right out. She waited inside for what seemed like a long time. Finally, she looked outside.

She laughed out loud at the three rear ends humped over the fender. The big one must have been Bill's.

Iris grabbed her purse and walked down the stairs and watched. He was patiently explaining to the boys what a distributor was, where the spark plugs were. He tapped a couple things with a screwdriver, went to the driver's seat, turned on the ignition, and the car started immediately.

Gray faced her with his hands on his little hips, leaning to one side as he always had since polio. "Gee, Mom, didn't you know you have to clean off the battery cables with baking soda and water? Gosh, everyone knows that."

Iris laughed. Gray had never seen a car battery in his life.

She said, "Well, I guess you've just got a silly mother, don't you?"

Bill was tall and heavy, but solid. Like a farm boy grown up. About her age, with an easy smile. His eyes never left hers.

Iris was grateful and opened her purse, but Bill wouldn't take any money for the work. "I see you every day walk out of Grimm's. Meet me at Woolworth's after work and buy me some coffee tomorrow."

Iris was suddenly flushed, surprised at her sudden emotion.

Where Bunny had been small and handsome like Alan Ladd, Bill was big like Broderick Crawford. But she was attracted to him, was impressed by the way the boys responded to him, and flattered that a man had been watching her all this time without her knowing.

She said yes, as Ida looked on, her eyes darting from Iris' to Bill's. The boys glanced at Iris, then at Bill, then at Iris, then at Bill.

Ida was still looking at her as she started the car and they all drove off on their adventure. Jimmy looked out the back window. Gray leaned over the front seat, and watched Iris operate the three pedals with two feet. He suddenly felt deflated, thinking he couldn't possibly do that, but said nothing and joined Jimmy at the back window.

The next day Iris made sure her favorite lipstick was in her purse as she left for work. Ida stared at her back as she left the house but said nothing.

A few weeks later, as Iris and her mother were doing the dishes, Ida looked down at her daughter's hand as she carried over a pan of hot water from the stove to the sink.

"So, you've stopped wearing your wedding band," Ida said. "I suppose I know what that means. You're getting ready to leave me again."

"Yes, Mother, if Bill asks me to marry him I will." She dried her hands and braced herself against the wall. "I want someone to lean on and I like caring again. The boys should not be raised by women. They need a man. I can't control them anymore."

Iris welcomed the relief in saying what she had been holding in.

"Mother, you were there when I needed you, and I won't forget that. I have to move on. But I would never move away from town like I did before."

Ida wouldn't give up. "What does a bachelor know about raising two boys?"

Iris laughed. "Please. You've seen how excited the boys are when Bill comes over, and he's excited seeing them, too. That is not even an issue. And you know, I've been taking care of the boys while Bunny was overseas, and ever since he died. Is it selfish for me to want someone to take care of me for a change?

"No, I don't love him like I did Bunny. Bunny was my first love. But Bill is a loving man."

"Well, see if he asks you to marry him," Ida finished.

In two months Iris and Bill were married and on their honeymoon at the Ozarks. She remembered to thank Muriel for her advice before they left.

Two days before the wedding, though, Iris drove her mother and the boys downtown to the theater for an Abbott and Costello movie. She knew the kids' grandmother wouldn't mind because Ida laughed at Abbott and Costello more than anybody. But Iris had to be alone for a few hours.

She walked out the back door, down the stairs, sat on the grass and tucked her legs under. She opened an old shoebox stuffed with letters. She slowly and lovingly read each of Bunny's letters to her from New Guinea.

Tears fell as she thought and remembered that other life, and looked into the sky. She smiled some and then cried some more. She separated the little photos from the letters and placed all the letters back in the box and put the top back on. She placed the box in front of her.

She reached into her breast pocket and pulled out a kitchen match. She struck it on the bricks surrounding the burn pile and held it to the edge of the box. Then she burnt it.

As the orange flames leapt and spread, she talked to the Bunny in the photos. He would always be young and skinny and handsome in his uniform.

"Oh, that smile," She said aloud.

"I'm getting married, soon, Bunny. He's a good man, and I do love him. It's not like my love for you. You were my first love and I thought you would be my last love. But he's a really good man. He adores me. He loves our boys, too."

Iris looked at the photo of Bunny sitting on the wing of a plane used in a raid in Darwin. How he hated those months and years in New Guinea and the humidity and the boredom. The Pacific waters were too warm to cool off in, and were throbbing with jellyfish.

The fire was out. She poked at the ashes with a stick.

She stood up.

"*Remember the past,*" she told herself. "*Don't dwell on it.*"

She walked back into the house. She carried four photos, the only legacy for Jimmy and Gray.

Chapter 5

$$1955$$

The new house in the country was small, two bedrooms and one bath, with knotty pine in the boys' bedroom. Iris and Bill were slowly working on the basement for an office and a family room. It was perfect.

After they moved in, she laughed at Gray's reaction to the finished bathroom. He was in awe at the shiny white bathtub.

"It's just beautiful, Mom!" He hadn't had a real bath since living at the Virginia farm. "I'm going to take a bath every day." The vow lasted three days.

They lived in a paradise for the boys. Besides their own yard of elm, oak, cherry, apple, and peach trees, a woods across the street was full of birds and snakes and rabbits. In the spring as farmer Kelly tilled the nearby soybean fields, Gray and Jimmy would follow close behind searching for and finding many arrowheads.

Since Gray no longer used crutches at all, his world broadened, although the heavy brace on his right leg sometimes left him breathless.

Iris knew the neighbors did not approve of her making Gray do chores around the house, but she felt she had to prepare him for the grown-up world.

She knew full well he would have to prove himself over and over in an intolerant world and there would be no special privileges for those who were not normal.

Her greatest confidence was knowing that the bad times were over. She knew that people may dread the hazards of life ahead, but she had paid her dues so there were no real bad times ahead like before. God could not be that cruel.

Maybe she gave Bill a hard time every now and then. It was difficult to relinquish the control she had had over her family for so long. But Bill was a kind man and was able to kid her till she had to laugh at herself.

However, Gray was becoming an angry boy. Sports were out of the question. It would be awful if he hurt his bad leg, a catastrophe if he hurt his good leg.

One morning Iris came into the boy's bedroom to clean up, and Gray was sitting on the edge of the bed watching the neighbor boys shoot baskets.

"Gray, what are you doing just sitting there?"

"Thinking," he replied.

"What about?"

"Things."

"Why don't you go out and play with the boys? It's too nice to be cooped up inside," Iris said.

"I don't want to. I don't care about them," Gray said flatly.

"Now, Gray, you've got to try," Iris said. "I didn't raise you to be a quitter." There was no comment. She walked out of the room with a cluck of her tongue.

That afternoon, as Iris was hanging the wash out on the line, her neighbor Vyetta approached.

"You can be sure I gave those boys a good talking to this morning, Iris," she said.

Iris dropped the damp shirt back in the hamper. "Boys?"

"Yes. Didn't you know? Gray come out first thing this morning and asked to play basketball and they told him to go away. That he wasn't good enough with his bad leg."

Iris put her hand to her mouth, and her eyes darted from side to side. It was though a felt like a fist had slammed into her chest. "You mean that happened this morning? Oh, Vyetta. Oh, my. I said something terrible to Gray this morning. I accused him of not trying to join in with the other boys."

"Oh, Iris!"

As Iris turned her head to watch Vyetta walk home she saw the curtain close in Gray's bedroom. He had heard it all. Now he was doubly humiliated.

Iris entered the room again, and sat on one bed facing Gray, who sat with his head down. She didn't know where to start. Hands in her lap, she twisted the gold ring.

"I..."

"Mom, why are people so mean to each other? It's not my fault I had polio."

His innocence, his fatigue with life, wounded Iris. She didn't know the answer.

Gray answered his own question. "Maybe people just don't like anything that's different from them. But there are lots of nice things about other people; but if you never give them a chance to show you, then...then...that's pretty sad."

Iris had never seen such strength from anyone in her life. Her throat caught at the knowledge that everyone needed respect, even a child. She hoped these experiences would not break him.

Together they walked into the kitchen.

Increasingly, Gray became sullen, moody. Iris missed the bright and happy boy he had been. She resented the world that punished a little boy for something over which he had no control.

It was late morning several days later when Iris and Gray drove towards town. In the distance, they could hear church bells. It seemed as though every church bell in town was tolling. And the fire siren went off. Horns began honking. Even the tornado siren started screaming though there was not a cloud in the sky, not a hint of wind. It should have been ominous, yet Iris felt like something wonderful had just happened.

It was after she parked the car that she saw the signs on the hardware store in crude, hastily-painted capital letters:

"THANK YOU, DR. SALK FOR INVENTING THE VACCINE!!! NO MORE POLIO!!!"

Iris squeezed Gray's hand, helping him up the curb, but saying nothing.

The next week, Iris yelled at him in the back yard. Rather than putting his brace on that morning he had thrown it flying into the middle of the raspberry bushes. Iris stood her ground, her demeanor rigid.

"Young man, you just go right in there and get that brace. Don't you want to get well?"

Scratched, and perhaps a little more grown-up, he crawled from underneath the thorny hedges, pulling the leg brace behind.

That afternoon she heard the taunts from outside the kitchen.

"Jimmy, come into this house. Now"

Jimmy was frozen in dread as he stood in the doorway.

"Stand against that wall and think about what you have just done."

She lit a cigarette, her eyes never leaving Jimmy's.

He knew he was in big trouble.

Moments slowly passed until she crushed out her Camel.

She smoothed out the faded blue apron. It was hers now.

"You're a handsome boy, aren't you? All that red hair. All your muscles in your arms. And your legs. Don't you know how lucky you are?"

Jimmy opened his mouth but she cut him off.

"What were those names you called your brother? PEGLEG? HOPALONG CASSIDY? How could you be so mean?"

Jimmy's eyes welled with tears. She cut him off again as he opened his mouth.

"Didn't our family learn anything from Gray having polio? Didn't we learn how just some bad luck can last the rest of our lives?" Tears rolled down his face.

She pointed her finger at him.

"I swear. If you ever torment him like that again, I'm going to get Bill's heaviest belt and teach you what a sore leg is like. DO YOU UNDERSTAND?"

He nodded. "I'll apologize."

"Jim, I know you want to go into the army like granddad and your dad. But part of being a proud man is respecting other people and understanding their weaknesses. If you don't care about people you are worthless, no matter what you may accomplish. Honey, I had to learn this, too.

"The only times I was in the hospital were when you boys were born. I had to learn and understand, too. Every mother wants her kids to grow healthy and strong. God knows, life is hard enough just being on an even keel. The first thing I did with you boys at the hospital was to count your fingers and toes and touch you all over to see if you were all right."

For the first time his mother was speaking to him as an adult, even at 12 years old. He swallowed his tears.

"I did it for Gray," he said.

Iris stared at him. "Explain that."

"Well, when kids tease him at school he starts to cry. Or he goes off behind a tree or something by himself. He should learn to fight. Sometimes I pop those kids, but I can't be around all his life. He has to learn to fight for himself."

Tears welled in Iris' eyes but she said nothing.

"I just figured that Gray is going to get so mad at me he'll start throwing a few punches. I know he can swing that brace hard when he wants to."

Iris didn't know what to say. She did not want her kids to fight. But she knew reality.

"Good. Good for you. I had no idea."

She looked out the window at Gray. He was lying in the grass looking into the sky. She wondered what rewards God could possibly have in store for him to make up for what He had done to him.

She looked back at Jim.

"You know, it wasn't too long ago I told you the difference between being smart and being wise was being able to interpret what you saw. You learned that lesson and I didn't."

"Well, he will probably end up hating me, but I think it's for his own good," Jim said as he started to the door to walk outside.

"Teach him to fight, but don't you dare call him names," Iris warned.

Before Jim could say anything, Iris heard Gray's words, "Stay away from me. I hope it happens to you. But I hope you get sick and you die."

She stepped outside.

"Boys, the three of us have to talk.

"Gray, Jim didn't go about it in the right way, I don't think, but he thinks you have to learn how to fight. And I guess maybe I do, too. Gray, I told you that people are really nice, and generally that's true but sometimes you have to make a stand. And Jimmy is going to try to teach you that. And I'm going to watch. Stand up."

Awkwardly, Gray stood up, and put his hands, now fists, in the same position Jim had taken. Jim pressed his hand against Gray's shoulder and Gray immediately collapsed. He started to sniffle.

"Gray, get up again," Iris said.

Gray stood up, wiped his nose and assumed a boxer's stance. He pushed against Jim's shoulder, but the mere unbalance made him fall again.

He continued to sniffle, embarrassed at his own weakness. He glared up at Jim.

"Well, I guess there's no such thing as a one-legged boxer," Jim said and shrugged.

With that, Gray grabbed Jim's heels and pulled them forward. This time Jim collapsed, and before he could get his wind back, Gray was on his chest, pummelling.

"Ow, my eye...ow, my ear...ow, my head...Mom, get him off me," Jim cried.

Finally, Jim stood up.

Gray laid still, grinning broadly.

"Well, maybe I can be a one-legged wrestler," Gray beamed.

Jim danced around, his fists shaking in the air in celebration.

"Manomanoman! Did you see him? He's like an attack dog! Wow!"

It was a turning point for the boy. He could compensate and adjust. He would never lose another fight.

As Gray stood up, she hugged the both of them and once again felt something very important had just happened to all three of them.

Iris was happy. Bill had gone from being a bachelor to becoming a husband and a father with no obvious effort. She assumed because of his large family, he liked bustle and commotion. He brought in $100 a week, enough money so she could quit her job to be a full-time housewife. She did not miss it at all.

Iris insisted the boys keep their father's surname, though. It was part of their heritage and their grandparents insisted on it. The boys wrote regularly to their Grandparents in Virginia because Iris didn't want the boys to lose that part of the family.

As regular as clockwork, a check for $25 would arrive from them for the boys' birthdays and also for Christmas.

Every other week Iris' family and Muriel's family would get together, the adults playing cards and drinking beer, the boys playing together, playing board games, arm wrestling or watching TV.

Iris and Bill believed in volunteer work. Considering the money the March of Dimes had given for Gray, Iris had joined their county organization and soon became the president. She felt it was another obligation she was happy to fulfill. She helped organize the Walk fundraiser when mothers would spread out through the neighborhoods in the evening, stopping at homes which had their porch light on, signaling they wanted to make a contribution. Often the city fire alarm would sound, alerting people to the mothers' march. Gray loved to see her name and picture in the paper, and wondering if he would accomplish the same.

Bill helped start the Reading Township Volunteer Fire Department for their remote area and became the Chief. Their lives were busy with the fundraising fish fries, friends, meetings, and summer vacations near beautiful Silver Lake in Wisconsin.

They were a respected couple, and any mother who knew Iris held her in special esteem.

Bill was a good mechanic, and a genuinely nice guy. He never openly ridiculed customers for their bad care of their cars. He did tell Iris about the time their neighbor Mrs. Kelly came in complaining about how much gas her car used. His thorough inspection found nothing wrong. The next time she came in with the same complaint, he asked her to take him for a drive.

She sat with Bill next to her and started the car, straightened her dress, adjusted the rear view mirror, and fluffed her hair. Not quite finished, she pursed her lips, outlined her eyebrows with the tip of her finger, and blinked twice.

He turned his head away for a moment, thinking, *"Women. We're just going around the block."*

She straightened her dress again and perked the collar.

"All righty then," she said.

Finally settled, she pulled out the choke lever to its full extent. Unconcerned at the noisy, racing engine, she hooked her purse strap around the lever and placed the car in first gear.

Bill told her to stop. He had found the problem.

———

One night at dinner Bill noticed the odd silence. The boys weren't talking or needling each other.

"OK, you two. What's going on?"

Jim started. "We think we deserve an allowance."

A half-smile passed between Bill and Iris. "You two want me to give you part of the money I work for all week? How do you figure that?"

"We mow grass and dry dishes and shovel snow," Gray said.

"Well, ain't that part of being a family? Don't you think your mother and I work around the house?" Bill let that sink in, and then let them off the hook as they looked down at their plates in silence.

"You can't expect money and jobs to come to you. You have to go out and work for money. You've got two good arms and legs."

He looked at Gray as Gray opened his mouth.

"Don't say it. You've got something more important than two good legs. You got a brain," Bill said. "Why don't you do those things for the neighbors?"

"Yes," Iris said. "You pick all those daisies and sunflowers from the field across the street for me. I bet the neighbors would pay 50 cents a bunch for them. Only you two know where that asparagus patch in the woods is. You could sell them. In the fall, I could drive you down to the riverbed to pick bittersweet branches to sell. And you could share a paper route after school. And shovel walks in the winter." She tried to excite them with her enthusiasm. The boys' eyes lit up as they imagined unlimited wealth.

They split a paper route, riding their bikes in the neighborhood, tossing out the afternoon paper after school. Gray answered an ad in a comic book, and sold Christmas card orders to his customers. There was hardly a flower left in the field that wasn't picked and sold. No doubt many of the neighbors learned to keep the curtains shut when Jim or Gray walked up the driveway carrying anything. Maybe Gray even learned to drag his leg a little more as the wives peered out to see who was out there.

At the end of two months, Iris was pleased with Jim. He had bought himself a bat and glove. However, Gray just seemed to spend all his money, with nothing to show for it. But it was his hard-earned money and she didn't ask about it.

It was when she was cleaning their bedroom that she found the bankbook. Gray had opened a savings account at 3.5% interest at the bank downtown with $11. He had saved $72. She was astounded.

Just then, Gray walked into the room, saw Iris sitting on his bed with the passbook in her hand and grinned. Yes, he was proud of himself.

Iris extended her arm out to him. "You saved all this money!"

He put on his Mr. Grizzly voice and touched her forehead with his. "I-I-I willl beee a rich mannn and you will beee a greaat laaady."

Iris hugged him and rested her cheek against his. She remembered those words on that train so long ago.

Also, Gray had started a hobby. Bill and his Grandfather Jim had given him foreign coins from China, Russia, Africa, Europe, and France that they had saved during the wars. Iris and Jimmy had hung a map of the world above Gray's exercise table and she had explained about the golden onion domes in Russia, and the Eiffel Tower and the big waterfalls in South America.

She tried to explain what a kangaroo looked like (like a big rat but nice, with a pouch in front for her baby) and told him his father had visited Australia several times during the war, and said it was a country where a man could begin a new life. All that might be waiting for Gray if he could walk well enough. It was a lifetime lesson for the boy.

"What would you like to see most of all, Mom?" Gray asked.

Iris considered the question.

"Well, every girl wants to see Paris, and I did too, but you know, all those years growing up at Gram's with that silver and green wallpaper with all those palm trees, I guess all I want to see is a palm tree! I think they are the most perfect and graceful tree there is! Isn't that silly?"

Gray considered her answer.

He would lie on the living room carpet and sort them as Bill and Iris read. A television wasn't part of their household yet.

He sorted them according to the country, admiring each one. One had a square hole in the middle, one had blue and green enamel. Another had funny writing with a sliver of a moon. He put that under "unknown."

"I like money," Gray said as he studied Bill's globe to match the country and the coin.

"Oh, we already figured that out," Bill said, making Iris laugh.

"Boyoboy, this coin is really, really old. It was made in 1918," Gray said.

Iris laughed. "So was I, honey."

Gray looked at her and then the coin in his hand, then back to her. "Wow."

He studied two coins in particular, and then brought them over to Iris and Bill.

"This is from England." He showed them a heavy bronze, 12-sided coin. "It's called three-pence. This is from Greece. I forget what it's called," and he showed them a bright silvery, lightweight coin. I bet England is a richer country because their coins are more impressive."

Iris and Bill smiled at each other. Gray went to the pile of coins and returned with several more.

"And this is where I am going." He showed them a franc, a ruble, a lira. "I'm going to these countries. But I have to get this brace off first, so I have to do my exercises extra hard."

Iris and Bill were extraordinarily pleased with their ambitious son when they went to bed that night.

Chapter 6

1957-59

Gray's ambition had to be put on hold for quite a while. It was time for a leg operation. His "good" leg was growing much faster than his "bad" leg. If his leg were not shortened he would have to wear a lift on the shoe of his braced leg the rest of his life.

The family entered the Peoria hospital room. It was on the 4th floor, and Gray was awed to be so high in the sky. He went straight to the window to look down, trying to find the top of their car.

There were three other boys about the same age: George, Al and Larry. Gray looked at them and at their braces lined up in the corner. He realized they were all soldiers in the same war.

Some time ago, Iris decided that it would be best if Gray was not around handicapped children, for he would see a reflection of himself. If he was only with normal people, she felt, he would feel more normal. It was an assumption she did not mention to anyone else. Maybe, just maybe though, she didn't want to see in the other children her own handicapped son.

The first hospitalization was when he had surgery on a toe, at the age of six. He had to wear a full leg cast for weeks. He was now eleven.

A lot of the repressed memories of that first visit suddenly rushed back as Gray heard the echoes, and the sound of metal beds, the smell of medicine, the smell of old food and bedpans. He remembered the long, long nights, and the other kids crying. He remembered saying to the boy in the next bed, "But we'll have fun here. And our family'll be back tomorrow," while fighting back his own tears.

He remembered Diana, who had been down the hall from him. Her parents were not allowed in the isolation ward, and the nurse didn't tell her they were outside trying to find the right window to wave to her. The only thing that soothed her after her parents left was clutching her Raggedy Ann doll. But then the night nurse grabbed it out of her hand.

"That's got polio on it. We have to burn that," she said, and pulled the doll from Diana's hands. She was inconsolable as Gray sat in his wheelchair next to her just to be with her.

—⟨∞⟩—

It was an awful time for everyone as Bill, Iris and Jim prepared to leave. Gray burst into tears, then Larry started to whimper, then the other boys. They knew from their own experience what it was like to be left in the hospital as the family left, and they were in complete sympathy for Gray.

"I'm sorry I had polio. Please don't leave me here. I'm sorry!"

Iris whispered in Gray's ear, "You are the bravest boy I know. You can do this."

Iris cried all the way back to Hardscrabble. Bill's heart was in his mouth. Two of the most important people in the world to him were hurting and, as big and powerful as he was he felt helpless.

The two nurses on the ward that night sat together in the lounge sharing a sandwich and a smoke. "All those boys crying for their families last night. It's so sad. Except for Gray. He just lies nice and quiet. That's good."

"No," said Jeri. She thought of her many years in dealing with children. "That's not good at all."

The Mondys couldn't return the next day, but had to be there the following day as that was when surgery was scheduled. Iris was anxious the entire time and barely spoke during the seemingly endless drive. She had Bill drop her off at the entrance before he parked the car. She walked quickly inside, knowing Gray would be nervous and scared.

To her amazement, there was laughter coming out of the room. When Iris walked in Gray said, "Mom, guess what dumb old Larry did!" Iris kissed him on the lips and said, "What did dumb old Larry do?" She sat next to him and smiled at Larry.

"That big Nurse Emma came in. We call her 'Nurse Enema.'" He laughed. "She came in and asked everyone when their last bowel movement was and Larry told her the TRUTH." Gray squealed all over again as she studied Larry lying on his stomach, miserable and embarrassed from the procedure.

Gray had learned years earlier you say, "Oh, I just had one" and never, ever: "the day before yesterday."

"Larry's a dummee," the boys started to chant. The other parents started to arrive and the kidding stopped suddenly.

Then Gray started to whisper:

"Mom, last night the guys and I were kidding with George. He's so little we were kidding him and I called him a squab. But today when his family came to take him home he told them I was calling him names. His Mom just came over and stared at me. I put the sheet over my head she looked so mad. But I was just kidding. Just like Jim and I do."

Iris knew immediately what the problem was.

"George is a black boy. When he told his mother you were calling him names, she probably thought you called him a nigger."

"A nigger? What's that?"

"Oh, it's just a name that's not very nice now for colored people. At one time it didn't mean anything too terrible, but now people made it ugly."

Gray was still baffled. "But what's wrong with somebody being colored?"

She sat closer to him on the bed and held his right hand. "When some people aren't very happy inside with themselves they make fun of others, sometimes when it's nothing that can be helped."

"Oh," Gray suddenly understood. "Like when Teddy called me a cripple right before I popped him!"

"Yes, and sometimes people like that need to be popped."

"But why didn't she just ask me?" Gray said. "He left this morning and she'll always think I called him a bad name and be mad at me."

"Oh, Gray," she said, shaking her head. "Practically all the problems in the whole world could be solved if people would just talk to each other. Sometimes people think something wrong and it just grows and festers, when nothing was meant at all.

"You know, some people don't like Jewish people, but it was a Jewish doctor who invented the Salk vaccine. Now no more little kids will ever get polio."

Gray paused. "Well. Why are people like that?

"People are the way they are. Sometimes people change." She thought of herself. "And sometimes they don't."

When Iris and Bill left for a cafeteria lunch, Gray thought and thought. He wondered what kind of world awaited.

Gray, moaning and sick from the ether, was rolled out of surgery toward evening. The doctor said it was all normal.

But the weeks in the hospital would gradually change his character forever. Iris noticed it first. He would not always look directly in peoples' eyes. His smile was not as broad or innocent, and she had studied that face since the moment he was born.

Sometimes he talked to his family while not looking at them at all, even looking out the window as they said "goodbye."

Iris wondered if he would grow out of it, and decided to talk to the head nurse, because she knew Jeri had spent a lot of time with Gray. She had once given Gray 35 cents to call home when he was lonely.

Several times in the car on the way home, she studied Gray's face. She was very troubled.

His leg always had to be elevated so as to not tear the sutured muscles in his knee. Bill had to carry him everywhere. Iris would carry an empty milk bottle in case he had to use the bathroom but could not get there without help. He felt humiliated. She and Bill talked long into the night on how to help him.

"Well, his cousins come over, and his friends from school. But they don't want to sit down and play checkers or talk. They want to go out running around."

"Yeah, and Gray just watches from the window," Bill said.

Iris nodded. "He's bright. We have to keep his mind busy."

Two days later Bill threw a heavy book on Gray's bed.

"You might as well have something to read," he said.

Gray looked down at the first volume of the World Book Encyclopedia A-E. He didn't look back up at Bill or ask what it was.

He lay on his side and opened the cobalt blue book as Bill left the room. When Iris looked in later he was still reading.

It worked. "The finest emeralds come from Columbia" he announced one night at the dinner table, half-facing the table as his leg was extended sideways on another chair.

Bill and Iris laughed aloud.

"You are screwy," Jimmy said.

And Gray had seen wonderful pictures of Australia. "Oh, to live next to the ocean," Gray had thought. By now he knew everything about Australia and decided to visit there one day.

At first, Iris and Bill humored him by asking what he had learned during the day, just for conversation. But after a while, they were rather interested in the facts, and Gray liked telling people about things they didn't know. It would pay off well.

Iris felt it was an important time for him so she bought a journal where he wrote everything down. At first he resisted, saying only girls keep diaries, but when Iris explained that all explorers keep journals, he relented.

He did not leave that out to be found as easily as the savings passbook had been. He made another decision: He would become a writer.

Iris was writing, too. Although she usually would fire out a letter on the standard Royal typewriter in their office basement, she knew this one had to be handwritten.

She had beautiful, careful, cursive, back-sloped writing. Her friends knew she would use only a fountain pen because Iris thought a ballpoint was "just a little ordinary-looking."

They would buy her fine notepaper, invariably with a colorful iris or two winding down the left side.

The letter began, "Dear Jeri, I do hope you will forgive my thoughtlessness at your sensitive suggestions about Gray..."

Iris had been pensive on the way back from the hospital because of the conversation she had had with Jeri. The nurse asked Iris if she could talk frankly, and Iris sat back in her chair as she began to realize how serious this conversation would be.

Jeri was older than Iris, with her hair pulled back severely in a bun. Her plainness gave her a kind of authority. Her rose-tinted glasses were quirky enough to relax her charges in the ward.

"Iris, my husband and I love kids, but we can't have any, so I guess that's why I get so involved in the kids in this ward. I've dealt with polio cases for probably 15 years now and I've made some observations.

"I don't have to tell you what a prize you have in that little boy. But there are some things you have to know." Iris stiffened at this woman giving her advice on a child not her own.

"I've noticed you call Gray's polio leg his "bad" leg. Iris, 'bad' has a bad connotation." She half-smiled. "It is not a bad leg. It is a weak leg. Gray or anyone else can't think it is bad.

"Did Gray ever tell you about his friend, Bobby?" Jeri continued.

"Yes," Iris said. "He had his legs broken when a tractor rolled over them."

Jeri hesitated and continued again. "Gray was always so proud that a teenager would ask him to come over to his room so they could watch 'I Love Lucy' together. Gray was over there every morning right at 9 in his wheelchair.

"And Gray hasn't talked about him? And you haven't asked?" Jeri asked.

"No," Iris said, somewhat defensively.

"Bobby's legs weren't broken, they were crushed. He finally had to have both amputated. He was moved to another hospital. Gray was devastated. It's not right that Gray shouldn't have talked about that, that he would keep that inside of him."

Jeri squirmed a bit in her chair as she noticed Iris' fixed expression but continued. "Another thing. People absolutely should not tell Gray that he's not normal. Again, that is a bad connotation. Disabled people are a normal part of life. He'll remember every day for the rest of his life he's not normal."

She wanted to comfort Iris. "The only thing about Gray that's not normal is the extraordinary courage he has."

It sounded like a platitude. Iris looked away.

"I know you are raising Gray to do things around the house, like Jim. And that was wise. But don't think Gray's experiences won't make his feelings or thoughts different from Jim or you or his cousins. They are too profound. I guess it's like being raised by an alcoholic as compared to a regular parent. It does affect a person." Jeri was startled when Iris suddenly stood up, and realized she had inadvertently tread on bad ground.

"Gray will be just fine, Jeri. Just leave that psychological stuff to me." She left the room, with Jeri still sitting in the chair.

———∞∞∞———

Iris finished the letter to Jeri and mailed it immediately. They were to exchange Christmas cards for many years once Iris had explained her feelings: "I just want everything I do to be the best for my boys, and I have to accept the fact that I make mistakes.

"But not everyone has a true friend who will tell her if some things aren't right. And you are my friend, and Gray's friend."

Time passed.

The boys grew in their own ways. In spite of the last operation, Gray would be taller than Jim, who loved sports and excelled at track and football

Iris and Bill were busy with their many friends and their community work. If at one time or another, Iris felt bushed by her family, social and civic responsibilities, she would watch Gray as with difficulty, but without a complaint mount stairs or the ladder to clean out the leaves from the drain spouts. Without consciously being aware of it, she was learning from her son.

---⟁---

It was a dangerous thought, but Iris couldn't help it: She was thinking "what if?" She had received a long letter from her friend "Crummee" from DC. Crummee had married the senator and wrote of the big house, the country clubs, and the trip to London.

Iris took out a small cedar box from the back of an old desk she and Bill had bought at a sale and refinished. In the living room, she pulled back the drapes to check on Gray and Jimmy playing catch in the front yard and then drew them close together. She would be alone for a while.

In the box were her first wedding ring, an opal pin, an opal ring, a ruby ring, and a delicate filigree gold bracelet with four round blue topaz settings.

She held the opal pin to the sliver of light coming through the drapes, and admired its fiery colors. She later learned it was called a black opal because of the depth of color and the lightning flashes of red, gold and blue. It was from Australia, a place called Coober Pedy she would find out years later. A young sailor she dated had given it to her when she lived in Washington.

"Iris, I'm going to Pearl Harbor, I'll be on the Arizona and will bring you back a pearl, but take this in the meantime," he had said.

"How long will you be in Pearl Bay?" she asked. She had never heard of any place in Hawaii except Honolulu; nor she was to find out, had most people at the time.

"Pearl Harbor, honey. I will be there for a year. Until about January of '42."

He never made it back. Instead, she had met Bunny that January. He was so handsome in his uniform that all the girls in the typing pool had stopped and stared when he walked into the War Room. He was tall with a boyish look, very thick auburn, unruly hair he vainly tried to comb straight back, and big brown eyes. That was how he got his childhood nickname, Bunny, from those big soft eyes.

He casually glanced around the room, aware of the attention, but he smiled only at Iris. And she noticed.

"Goodbye, Paris," she whispered to the girl next to her. That was the beginning.

She held the opal ring and slid it easily on her right ring finger. It had been hidden away but still shown brightly. This was a round, white opal, but with the same fiery veins of red, gold and blue. It was in an Art Nouveau rose gold setting, and eighteen karats. Bunny had given it to her for Gray's second birthday in October because opal is the birthstone. But a few weeks later when Gray fell ill with polio, Iris decided opals were as bad luck as she had heard. She took it off.

She put them in a black velvet bag in the back of the box.

Bunny was only first generation American, so he had the European love of fine jewelry. His father wore a pigeon blood ruby ring on his little finger. Iris at first thought it looked rather funny for a man to wear it on such a large, wide hand, but Bunny explained it had been his grandfather's and was worn in that style, and his father later gave it to Bunny. She would pass it on to Jim when he turned 21, like Grandfather Jim had.

Iris' one-carat engagement ring should have been in the cedar box, but Bunny had pawned it for a gambling debt. He was such a dreamer, always wanting the easy way to get rich, she thought. She remembered sliding it off, handing it to her husband, looking not at the ring, but in the eyes of the man she loved.

Later, Bunny gave her the bracelet to make up for the loss of her ring.

"What if Gray had never gotten sick? What if Bunny hadn't died?" The farm would be worth a fortune now. The kids' grandparents divided their time between Virginia and a house on Anna Maria Island, off the West Coast of Florida.

Iris let herself imagine, then cut herself off.

"Well, I wouldn't have met Bill, or became so close to Muriel, or have my friends in Hardscrabble."

Just then, Jim opened the front door and asked her if she wanted to play catch with him and Gray. She set the box down behind the base of the table lamp, and grabbed a headscarf.

As she closed the front door behind her, Gray threw the ball impossibly high. But somehow she was able to jump up, and with one hand caught the ball and landed on her feet. The boys shrieked with admiration and surprise.

"*This is better than any country club could ever be,*" Iris thought.

———

Iris was approaching 40 and she wanted to give Bill his own child. Mostly, things were still fine. Jim was excellent at school and was also a fine athlete, earning the name "Zip" because he could run so fast, slipping easily around any team's defense. He was small like her father, and sturdy. But whenever it was time for Gray's leg exercises he would go to the basement to work out with his weights. It was obvious to anyone he detested illness or weakness.

For her birthday, Bill took her to The Lodge at Starved Rock State Park. It was rather fancy with private bungalows and old, drooping trees. It was also rather romantic, and expensive at $24 a night, and overlooked a huge gorge and the river. Legend was that the Indians, starving, threw themselves off the ledge into the Illinois River.

Not too long after, Iris announced she was pregnant. She enjoyed the kidding because all her friends had kids who were teenagers, and 'the girls' all loved the idea of a baby to spoil.

A few weeks before her due date, Iris and Bill drove Gray to the orthopedic doctor in Peoria. Their visits were down to one about every six months, and Gray's brace had been cut down over the years from the belt-type, to one that ended at the thigh, and now to a calf brace. She knew Jim would think of some excuse not to go, so she didn't ask him.

Dr. Canterbury was about Iris' age. He seemed to hold Iris in high esteem because he never took his eyes off her when they spoke. His care for Gray was professional, yet personal.

As usual, Gray stripped to his underpants while Iris looked on. The doctor had Gray lie on his back while on the table, and measured the leg lengths from the hipbone to the ankle of each leg, and musculature of the calves and thighs. Gray turned over. He traced Gray's backbone to make sure there was no spine curvature. Gray had been poked and felt and examined for longer than he could remember, and was placid as usual.

This time, however, the doctor asked Iris to leave the room while he called in two other doctors for consultation.

Iris waited impatiently with Bill, sure that something wrong had developed in Gray's back from the years of favoring the weak leg. She hadn't smoked since she became pregnant and this was when she wanted a cigarette most. Bill sensed her strain and stared at the magazine in his lap, knowing any attempt at conversation was useless.

"*Why,*" she fretted, "*Why did I push him so hard?*"

When she was called back into the room Gray was dressed. The leg brace was lying on the floor. She was afraid to believe what her eyes were seeing.

"Gray's remarkable," Dr. Canterbury said. "He is a master of compensation. He uses his other limbs to compensate. We all agreed the brace is no longer necessary."

Iris rushed to Gray, hugging him hard. She was so happy she almost felt sick to her stomach.

"Gray, you are like a wolf," the doctor said. "A wolf that loses his toes in a bear trap, and has to use his cunning and intuition, and perfect the rest of his body to survive."

He paused.

"Remember this, though. It's one thing to be a cute, handicapped boy. It will be quite another to try to compete in business or romance with able-bodied men. Some people will try to best you by making themselves superior by putting you down. Just remember that's a weakness on their part, not yours. You wear your only weakness on the outside while others have theirs inside. You'll do it, but just remember it will not be easy."

He cleared his throat suddenly; aware that perhaps he was crossing the doctor/patient line by giving Gray advice on how to conduct his life.

"Your first doctor was Dr. King. He was a good doctor, and a kind man. Maybe too kind. I've been hard on you these years because I couldn't use sympathy for your not wanting to wear your brace, or those operations. Just be glad you're not a girl or those scars would show with a dress on.

"But I and your family and especially your mother helped you through this. Come back and see me in a year." All three shook hands.

Gray looked proudly at Iris.

Iris was definitely sick to her stomach now. She had to talk to Bill.

Bill stood up when he saw the expression on her face.

"Get me back to Hardscrabble. Something's wrong with the baby."

But sitting down in the car, and the warmth of her hands on her stomach helped. She caught her breath and told Bill of Gray's wonderful news. Bill sped off, while Gray sat in the back holding the brace. He cradled it, seeing 11 years of polio prison doors opening, and the world waiting.

Iris checked into the hospital because all tests showed the baby was going to arrive early. It was going to be big, because Bill was a big man. That had been what scared Iris; this pregnancy was different from her other two.

Three days later, with a Caesarian and a great deal of pain and a concern, Patrick was born at 7 pounds and 7 ounces. She took a lot of kidding on the hospital floor, with one son ready for his driver's license, and one son celebrating his 13th birthday while she held her newborn baby boy.

"So, does Bill get along with your other boys?" her hospital roommate asked when they were alone at feeding time.

"Oh, yes, he practically raised them."

"But they don't call him 'dad'?"

"No, I just felt it wouldn't be fair to their real father," Iris said. "But of course, Pat will."

Shortly after, Bill, Jim and Gray came to visit. Gray was horrified to see tubes running out of her nose and tubes running into her arms.

"That little kid better treat Mom right after all she's been through," he thought.

"Well," Iris said, "Two wonderful boys born on October 28th. We will have quite a celebration when we get back home."

"Another wonderful boy was born on October 28th, Mom," Gray said. "Jonas Salk was born that day."

"How did you...?" Iris began. Then she laughed. "You and those encyclopaedias!"

Chapter 7

---⦿⦿⦿---

1964

Mostly, they were all dead now. The devastation was almost incomprehensible for Iris.

She was taking the baby to show her big sister Leola in Kewanee. Pat was sleeping in his bassinet in the back and Iris was staggered by her thoughts of the factory girls.

All those pretty, happy girls from the watch factory, all in their twenties when Iris met them, with their fur-trimmed collars and dark eyes and fine shoes. They would only shop in Chicago, and only at the finest stores.

It was an avalanche of illness. Nausea at first, then one had a leg amputated. But then another her arm! Then one girl who was pregnant when she worked there had a little boy who later died of leukemia. Iris knew the guilt the woman would carry the rest of her life.

All the girls from the radium watch factory had cancer. They were "The Radium Girls."

That was when Iris' faith in doctors, the legal system and the corporate world was shaken. The company said it was broke, so there was no compensation.

For years, the company and its doctor denied there was any connection with the cancers and the work. She remembered Leola explaining that when the camel-hair bristles needed pointing to finely paint the radium on the dials the girls were told to wet them to a point with their lips. It was tasteless stuff. How could they have ever known? After all, wasn't radiation used to TREAT cancer, not CAUSE it? Wasn't that what Madame Curie had done? Iris wasn't sure, but that's what other people had said.

She borrowed a book from the library and learned what she could about the Curies. It finished when he was run over by a carriage on a street in Paris.

Leola was one of the few who had survived, and the cancer seemed under control. Iris thought it was the family's hardy Irish genes...that the people in their family may get sick, but they spring back. Except for her father who died of too much beer and bourbon, they always sprung back...even Gray.

Jim was a perfect, healthy teenager. Pat was a perfect, healthy baby.

It was ironic that Leola needed a leg brace now, and it was Dr. Canterbury who fitted her. Iris sometimes felt there was a plan somewhere, that life is a series of tests, that every happening is an instance not to be overlooked, but drawn on to prepare the person for the next.

Leola's children had all married young and moved away. Soon after Leola's husband died, she remarried and was happy in spite of everything. It was interesting to Iris that the tragedies she herself had experienced so young in life, others were experiencing now.

Back in Hardscrabble, every so often someone would phone and ask to speak to her privately. She provided the best advice. She simply sat and listened, never taking her eyes off theirs, until they seemed to work out the problem themselves.

She laughed once when she heard that the main answer of a psychiatrist was "Well, what do YOU think you should do?"

"I should have been a psychiatrist instead of a secretary," she told a friend.

The sisters talked of these things and of the future. It was their last time together.

Chapter 8

---❯❯❯❮❮❮---

1965-67

Gray and Jim were learning how invaluable a little brother could be. On Jim's visits home, they would argue about who took Pat out for the afternoon, whether it was a walk downtown or to Quarry Lake. Girls, charmed by the boy, always surrounded them. Naturally, Pat reveled in all the attention, and no kid grinned more than he did.

Gray had him trained perfectly when they met up with a particular girl: "Now when I wink, you say: 'Gee you're pretty!'" It was a perfect and loving conspiracy.

Iris was fascinated how three boys could be so different.

"*Three sons, one mother, and all so different,*" she thought. Jim, handsome, ruddy, and sturdy could be stern and disciplined, and looked like his father. Gray, handsome in a different way, with hazel eyes like Iris' seemed restless and easily disappointed in people. Pat, with his round face and bright eyes and curly hair was the happiest boy she had ever seen, and mature because of the direction of his older brothers. He looked like Bill and me both, Iris observed.

By now, Jim was a senior at Virginia Military Institute in Lexington, Virginia, studying physics and German. Because it was a prestigious school, one had to have the right connections and be a perfect candidate just to be considered. His grandfather had been a teacher there during World War II and Jim rallied to the strict discipline. He was the only one in all Illinois that was appointed, and Iris became a total bore when she bragged to her friends and family.

And of course, her friends didn't mind a bit in Iris having something wonderful to talk about after all the years of hardship.

Only once did it present a problem. She was on the phone to a friend.

"And there are three whole pages of how perfect his teeth must be before they would approve him! His body just has to be perfect. I'm so proud of him."

Out of the corner of her eye, she saw Gray round the corner and knew he had heard. He would always have a limp and she was ashamed of herself for hurting his feelings by bringing attention to something he could not help. She excused herself, hung up the phone and went to him.

"Gray, you know that had nothing to do with you."

"Look, Mom," Gray laughed. "Mom, let's not get paranoid about this. I am me. This is me."

Gray was a head taller than she was, and she pressed her head against his chest. It was thick and muscled. His years on crutches and the extensive use of his arms had made him exceptionally strong. Again, she remembered FDR and his powerful torso.

Gray had worked the last two years of high school as a bagger at the local supermarket after work and on weekends, and saved his money for college. The manager was a bit concerned that Gray may physically not be able to handle the stress, but Gray was an expert at substituting his arms or strong leg when the need came for lifting or for standing too long.

A year later at the "Bull Session" meeting after the store closed on a Friday night, the manager asked why the other baggers weren't as fast as Gray, "even with his bum leg." And the manager told Bill that his single-items sales by high school girls picked up on the days that Gray worked.

As the year neared its end, it was the last truly carefree Christmas for Iris. Although Bill was not a churchgoer, he had no problem attending the midnight High Mass that Christmas.

The church was warm and beautiful, with a vaulted, ornate ceiling. There were masses of red poinsettias on the white marble altar, hymns were sung, and the smell of evergreen garlands and incense was everywhere.

She led her entourage down the aisle, holding the hand of her bubbly little boy Pat, then Gray followed, then Jim, so distinguished in his gray VMI dress uniform with his girlfriend Sydney, the daughter of the brick factory owner, and then Bill.

As she knelt down, she glanced across the aisle at Mimi, who could hardly take her eyes off Gray. With Coco Chanel hair and doe eyes, she was one of the prettiest girls in town. She was even prettier tonight, with her mustard corduroy double-breasted suit with its big brass buttons. She had made it herself, and had decided to become a fashion designer. Of course, Iris remembered Mimi's mother saying that she went to every Mass on a Sunday in the hope of 'bumping-into' Gray.

Iris stayed kneeling as the others sat back. She had been a Methodist, but after Bunny died she became a Catholic so the boys could be raised completely in his religion. All these years she had attended church on Sunday, and always felt relief and confidence when she walked outside after Mass.

It had been a happy year for her. Jim was captain of the wrestling team and would be commissioned into the army in a few months after graduation. She worried about Jim and Vietnam and asked God if there was a way for Him to help Jim not go there. Gray attended Northern Illinois University, about an hour away studying journalism. The cobalt blue books and coins had paved the way for his future.

It was just the three of them at home now, and she was so glad they had Pat.

"Thank you, God, for giving me what I now have," She said quietly.

It had been a sad year for Gray. One of his closest friends, a strapping six-footer had been badly injured in an electrical accident, losing one arm and part of his feet when the hydraulic lift he was operating connected with high-voltage wires. The man who tried to save Ray by pushing him off the lift was killed, absorbing all the electrical energy himself.

Like Iris' friends, Gray's friends were starting to deal with the inevitability of accidents and illness and death. He spent the weekend on the farm with Ray after he was released from the hospital. The boys talked long into the night. Ray showed Gray the awful gash where the three toes and the side of the outer foot had been removed. Gray felt the hook that Ray would wear.

They both remembered just a couple months earlier, the night rides by the river, parking with their girlfriends and scaring each other with tales about "the hook man" who stalked parking teenagers. In the legend, the kids would hear a noise in the dark, speed off, only to find a hook in the rear bumper the next morning.

It was all too real and too sad for both. But Ray felt a lot better talking because Gray had understood.

And Gray had to face something, too. He remembered watching Ray play basketball and envied his strong legs so much. And it had come to this. After that, whenever Gray felt that life had not been fair to him, he had thought of Ray.

"*Everyone has his cross to bear*," Gray thought.

———⊗———

A few days after Jim returned to school he called home. There had been a wrestling accident and his knee was torn so badly he would be on crutches for month. The hopes of a career in the military were over. She knew this would keep him out of the army and keep him out of Vietnam. Maybe God had heard her prayer?

He described how he had to keep his leg elevated at all times so the suture would heal in his knee...just like Gray had done.

And it was the same leg that Gray had had his knee operation on. She felt an awful foreboding because Jim had never been in bad health. She dismissed it as an over-worried mother. She was wrong.

Graduation in Lexington, Virginia that June was thrilling with all the pomp and circumstance of an old military school. Jim's grandfather was bursting with pride that Jim was following in his footsteps.

It astonished Iris when she heard Grandfather Jim's comment to Gray, however, and she said furiously, "Don't you ever call Gray a cripple again."

With regret, Iris had to recall that Chinese dinner she had with Bunny the day she had met President Roosevelt. She had received her engagement ring earlier and they decided to go out to their favorite restaurant. Iris was ecstatic she had met the most important person in the world and mentioned the strength of his arm as she reached down to shake his hand.

"But Bunny...a man like that in a wheelchair. Polio is the most awful thing. I think I'd kill myself rather than go through life like that."

She wasn't proud of her arrogance and ignorance, her thinking that strength was only measured in muscles.

Gray had taught her so much since. But she resented that others felt as she had long ago, and that it reminded her of herself.

It was fortunate for Grandfather Jim that Iris hadn't heard him also say to Gray, "No girl could ever love you. They could only pity you."

In his military mind, all weakness was unacceptable. Iris was glad her kids had been raised away from that influence of his rigid and unaccepting domination. It was for that and other reasons she had to move away right after Bunny died.

Gray had been totally taken aback by the affront, but loved his grandfather and dismissed the slur as he remembered what Iris had told him that one day at the hospital about people who call other people names.

Nevertheless, the festivities were grand, and the weather as bright as Jim's future. Astronaut John Glenn gave the commencement address. There were hundreds of people and elegant cars, and the VMI band played stirring music from James M. Cohan. Iris laughed when two dogs got in a fight, and Pat said, "Shouldn't we call a police dog?"

As Jim stood at attention next to her she couldn't take her eyes off his face. He looked like Bunny so much. She inspected him, down from his clipped red hair, down to his forehead to his strong nose and chin.

Further down, though, her eyes caught on a mole, red and angry at the top of his stiff collar. She asked him about it immediately, but he said that because his best friend

Wayne and his best girl Sydney were there, he didn't want to bother with it. He promised to have it looked at later.

Within weeks there were job offers from all over the East Coast, but he passed on them and accepted a good job in Chicago for Continental Can company.

Later, at the dermatologist's office he met and fell in love with Pam, his nurse, also pale-skinned and red-haired. The mole was removed a month before the wedding.

It was on a Saturday that Jim unexpectedly arrived in Hardscrabble in his long, black Lincoln Continental. Gray happened to be home from college.

When Iris saw that his very pregnant wife Pam was not with him she could only stare. Her mother's intuition was screaming: "Something's wrong. Something's wrong."

The four sat in the kitchen to learn the horrible news. The doctor had not done a biopsy on the mole! Jim had melanoma, the deadliest form of skin cancer. Seed spores had spread everywhere and only possibly could operations and extensive chemotherapy help.

If not, he had only a few months to live. She and Bill watched the shiny black car drive away. To Iris it looked like a hearse.

"I hope there's an accident and he gets killed," she said.

Bill was aghast as he stared at Iris, his jaw dropped in amazement.

"Do you know what these next few months will be like for him?" she said, remembering the factory girls.

Gray didn't take it seriously at first. Jim had always been in perfect condition. It was impossible that he could become sick or worse. He would pull through, without a doubt.

Iris, however, knew too much about the unfairness of life. She sat on her bed and looked out the window. Dirty winter clouds were rolling in fast, obliterating the cobalt blue sky. Her mind went back to her mother's house and what she had said to the crucifix so long ago. *"What did I do? I told God…GOD! to leave my kids alone! Is He punishing me for my arrogance? Punishing me through Jim?"*

She thought some more. *"If I failed to protect Gray from polio, did I fail with Jim by letting him go out in the sun when he was little?"* She remembered her little shirtless Indian. All the kids in town went out half-naked during the summer. How does anybody keep a shirt on a boy in the summertime?

"Was I supposed to have learned something from Gray that I didn't? How was I to know the sun could feel so good and be so deadly?"

Gray was outside, conflicted in his thoughts.

"Could this be serious, after all?"

Then he remembered his own words, "I hope you get sick but I hope you die!" that he had yelled at Jim that one day. If he had earned grace from his suffering, and asked God for something, did God grant that awful wish? Certainly, God knew it was a child's anger, only to be dismissed, didn't He?

Bill walked slowly to the garage, pulled a spade off the wall, and tightened it in the vice. He got out the file and slowly sharpened the blade. It was a completely useless gesture, as the ground was like concrete that time of the year.

Pat was in the back yard, peeking around the edge of the garage at the back door. Although he had been told to go out and play, he, too, knew that something awful was befalling their house.

A monster was lumbering toward their little home on Jackson Street, and everything would change forever.

Chapter 9

1968

The months of January, February and March were the worst of Iris' life. Jim and Pam moved in with them since the hospitals could do no more.

Four adults, one child and one on the way, one bathroom. The house was too small. Jim moaned constantly from the pain. They were housebound due to the wintry weather.

Once there was a terrible scene at the hospital when Jim's wife screamed at the head nurse when Jim was refused any more medications.

"For Christ's sake! My husband is dying! Who the hell cares if he becomes addicted?"

It was the first time Iris had seen authority questioned. She not only agreed with Pam but she wondered how many other times in her life had she gone along with a decision just because the person was more powerful.

"Fuck, fuck, fuck" Jim cried out in pain one afternoon as he lay in bed. Bill marched to the door of his bedroom and yelled at him not to swear with women in the house. Iris was furious and lashed out at Bill under her breath.

"Oh, Bill let him cuss all he wants! Doesn't he have a right to? He's 24 years old and dying! Don't we all have a right to scream and cuss!"

"Get out," Jim said. "Just leave me alone." They left the room.

He was absolutely bewildered at the betrayal of his body. He thought: *"It's like everything I avoided about Gray has come to me...the wheelchair...people helping me to the toilet. Even Gray helping me."*

They all had had to learn to give Jim pain shots, practicing on an orange. "Take the hypo gingerly between your thumb and index finger and poke sharply into the flesh. Do it boldly or you will have to dig deeper and it will hurt," the doctor explained. "And pull back on the plunger to see if there is blood in the syringe. If you put air into the vein it will kill him." Iris sickened.

Iris could not bring herself to do it till one day she was alone with Jim and he was crying with pain. She was making herself sick, blaming the doctors for everything. She wondered why only her children got sick. She wondered why everything happens to her. She could talk to God no longer.

But she talked to herself: *"What was the point of taking his gall bladder out for God's sake? That's an old man's illness! What did it do but make him more sick? Why can't they give him more morphine? Are they worried he'll become an addict before he dies?"* Pam was right to fight.

Again, she was with a desperately ill son. But instead of a young boy getting better, it was a young man dying.

She could take no great pleasure in the birth of her grandchild. She had to ask what would be waiting in this world except suffering, pain and death? The baby wouldn't have a father, just like Jim and Gray all over again. Her doctor prescribed blood pressure pills for her, and they did help because she knew she had to care for Jim as best she could

She looked into the mirror. Her greatest physical assets, she thought, were her tiny figure and thick black curly hair. In the last few weeks her hair had started to gray. It was lopsided, unkempt. She remembered Mrs. Armour so long ago. Her face was drawn, too. But she was nearly 50 and still attractive. She only wore a bit of lipstick now, though, in an attempt to make her life as un-beautiful as possible.

Her girlfriends had stopped asking her to bridge or to lunch. Iris did not want to find any pleasure in life if her oldest son could not, and refused all social activities.

She was angry at Bill. His stoic attitude proved he really didn't love Jim. Every time there was a turn for the worse, all he did was reach for his pipe, load it and light up, and walk out of the room. She wondered if she should take Pat and move out after it was all over.

And this time it was Gray's turn to be off put by illness and infirmary. On his visits home he would excuse himself for an hour or so to lift weights or swim at the local YMCA.

Unfortunately, Jim's wife Pam was virtually ignored when friends and neighbors called by. Since they all knew Iris, people rushed to her.

The social aspects of visiting were overshadowed by the immensity of the situation. Pam began to rebel.

"I hate this house. I hate this town," she screamed to Iris one day.

Iris stood her ground. "Our family has had many years of happy times in this house and in this town. Don't you judge everything by the last few months."

It was the old story about two women, two generations under the same roof, each wanting their own territory. Iris had to think of her and Bunny and the boys and her in-laws back on the farm. And her years with her mother.

But it was no one's fault, and they would realize that later.

Pam's joy at the stirrings of her first child was overshadowed by the approaching death of her young husband. But as a nurse, she had studied homeopathy and she had to think what the chemicals and hormones from her worry were doing to her unborn baby. She tried to remove herself more and more from the day-to-day ordeal.

One morning, Gray took Jim to the toilet, lifted him from his wheelchair, pulled his pants down in the bathroom and started to leave. It was Jim's turn to be humiliated.

"You don't know what it's like, being in a wheelchair, being lifted up and carried around," he yelled at Gray's back. Gray turned and looked at him.

"Well." It was the only word Jim could utter for several seconds. "I guess you do." Then, "I just didn't know how bad it was."

He corrected himself. "I did know. That's why I hated to be around when Mom gave you your leg exercises. I knew they hurt. And I hated it when the doctors kept poking at you."

"And I thought it was me you hated then," Gray said.

"Jim, just learn to be patient with yourself. Learn to know what you can do and don't worry about asking other people for help. Don't you think they want to help you? They need to know they're doing something for you."

Gray sat in the wheelchair to be on eye-level with his brother. There is no room for modesty in illness.

"Ok," Jim said. "So I should ask Mom for help even when I don't really need it, just so she thinks she's helping?" he asked.

"It would mean everything to her," Gray said as he stood up.

"And you didn't treat me so bad, Jim. You taught me to fight," Gray said. "Now it's your turn."

About a half-hour later Jim called out from his bedroom: "Mom, could you do me a favor?"

In an instant Iris was at his bedside wiping her hands on that old blue apron. "Of course, honey. Anything."

"I didn't want that milkshake this morning, but it sure sounds good now. But could you make it chocolate? And put a couple eggs in it?"

"Sure, honey. Sure." She rushed to the kitchen, barely able to see the blender to crack the eggs into, blinking the tears back furiously.

How many meals had she prepared in that little kitchen? Thousands. Yet this meal was the most important ever.

She remembered Gray and Jim as boys, almost breathless watching her make fudge on a Saturday afternoon. And then the lengthy debates about who would get the wooden spoon and who would get the mixing bowl to lick. Each was sure the other got more.

And the smells of frying chicken, and the Sunday roasts after church. Gray on a chair whipping the potatoes for Sunday lunch. The clink of the buckshot in the bowl as they feasted on a pheasant or a rabbit Bill had shot. Such trivial things. Such important things.

She added her secret to the chocolate shake bubbling in the blender: a tiny pinch of black pepper.

The day was going to be very busy for Iris as she was to meet Muriel downtown and take care of the necessary arrangements for what would happen to Jim. Iris hadn't noticed at first that Pat was calling her name.

Finally, she looked down and saw a very bewildered and lonely child with his hands cupped in front of him poking at her legs.

"I know what would make you happy, Mom. Look, it's a robin's egg." He opened his hands and the little blue orb lay there.

Without saying a word she went to the phone.

"Muriel, something's come up and I want to postpone everything until tomorrow. Yes, everything's fine." She hung up.

In one overwhelming moment Iris realized what she had done; practically ignoring this little boy who was feeling everything she did but had not the maturity to deal with it. Was she putting Jim over Pat the way she put Gray over Jim?

"Let's take it outside and see if we can find its mother. I bet she's looking for it." She reached for a saucepan. "But I think we should have some cocoa to keep us warm, don't you?" Pat beamed.

They sat at the base of the thick oak tree, watching the egg about 15 feet away, the steaming cups in their hands. They sat on one end of an army blanket and tucked the other end over their laps.

At that moment, Vyetta was walking out the back door to bring over a sour cream coffee cake for Iris and her family. As she turned to close the door, she saw Iris and Pat. The women's eyes locked only for a moment but it was enough.

Back inside, Vyetta laid the cake down and took off her coat. She said to her boys, "I don't want you two going over to play with Pat or even calling him on the telephone. This is a family day for them." She took out her hanky from her breast pocket and blew her nose.

Iris began, "You know, Pat, that when a mother bird knows one of her babies is in trouble somewhere she will leave the others to look for the one that needs her the most. Maybe that's what I've been doing with you since Jim got so sick." She hoped he would understand.

His head rested against her shoulder. "You said when Gray was little he got really sick but he got better even though his leg didn't get well. Maybe that's what will happen with Jimmy."

Pat was remembering Jim and him skinny dipping at the creek, and the sheriff yelling at them that they were on private property and him making them walk away before they could put on their clothes, and Jim holding him on his lap teaching him to drive that big Pontiac, and Jim taking him to that dark and smoky pool hall and how mad Mom got.

"Well, whatever happens you know that dad and Gray and I love you, and that will never change."

Iris thought that whatever mistakes she had made as a mother in her early years she had a chance to correct now.

It was as perfect an afternoon as possible. The pain had left Jim for a while and he was hungry. Iris, Pat, Jim and Pam had Campbell's tomato soup and grilled cheese sandwiches. They set up a card table with a jigsaw puzzle on it near his bed. An old sailing ship, sails unfurled gradually came to view as the last few pieces of a puzzle were added.

Iris remembered a poem that Gray liked, something by Edgar Lee Masters. Gray had said, "I don't want my life to be a ship with furled sail at rest in a harbor."

Jim was getting tired, but as he laid his head back on the pillow he said to Pam, "Is that the ship that Gray is leaving on?"

Pam looked at Iris, who could only shake her head and slightly shrug her shoulders. She didn't know what he meant, either.

The next day the egg was gone. Pat was sure the mother bird had somehow carried it back to the nest. Iris convinced him it was so, even while she watched their red setter Corky sniff the ground where the egg had lain.

It was late afternoon when the doctors left after sitting with Iris alone for some time. The sun was about to set. She walked to Pat's room. He was sitting on the edge of the bed, a book on his lap, unopened.

She sat next to him and knew that he knew, but she had to say it anyway. "Pat, the doctors say that Jim is going to die."

He smiled and forced hope out of his voice. "No, no, Mom. You just didn't understand them. What they really, really meant is that part of Jim would stay sick like Gray's leg when he got sick. But he'll be okay. You'll see."

"Pat, Jim is going to die. And you have to be brave."

He threw the book on the floor, yelling: "No, he's not! They're only people! What do they know about things like that? Only God knows that!" It was the indefatigable logic of a nine-year-old.

She knew in an instant more he would break down and Iris didn't want to make him feel embarrassed, to lose his pride. She simply kissed his forehead, left the room and closed the door.

Iris needed her sister, more than ever. They met for coffee.

The town knew about Jim, and the waitress grimaced and nodded to Iris in sympathy as she entered, then motioned her to the table where Muriel sat expectantly.

Iris smiled in Muriel's direction, shrugged off her coat, pulled off her gloves and sat down, avoiding Muriel's eyes till the last minute, afraid she would break down.

She waited for the cup to be filled, reached for her spoon and laid it back down again.

"I don't know. I think when this is all over I may leave Bill."

Muriel was stunned. "Why, my word, Iris, you don't know what you're saying! Why would you say that?"

"He doesn't care about Jim. Maybe he never did. I try to talk to him and he just fills his pipe and lights it up and walks away. He hardly ever says a word. It took me this long to find that out."

"Oh, Iris, you are wrong. Wrong. Bill's not like that," Muriel pleaded.

"Well, I'll decide in a few days. In a few days it'll all be over."

She reached for the spoon and watched the swirls form in the cup.

The baby girl was born on a Sunday, Jim held his daughter on a Thursday and he died on a Friday.

Iris thanked God that at the moment he had passed away, just as she was walking out of the room, she suddenly turned back to look at Jim and saw his life pass out of him. She had been able to rest her hand on his forehead. She had never felt so close to him. To be there at his birth and at his death moved her profoundly, and in a sense, completed her.

She walked into the living room. "Bill, Jim's gone."

Silence. Then a howl which she had only heard once in her life, the moment her dog had been crushed by the tractor, his life torn out from his lungs. But this time it was Bill!

He covered his face in his hands, and simply, bawled. Bawled. Iris was stunned, speechless.

Instantly, she knew. How could she have misjudged him so? To think he didn't love Jim! He had put on a brave front these past few months to help her. She should have known better. When Gray suffered so, she was a blank canvas, stoic to help him cope. Hadn't she learned anything? She put her hands on Bill's heaving shoulders till they calmed. He sat back in his chair, winded and completely unashamed.

Gray got the call at his apartment at college and drove back about midnight. Opening the front door, he had an awful decision. Should he go to Pam on one side of the room first or to his mother on the other side? Iris had known tragedy, Pam had not, he thought as he knelt down beside Pam. Muriel and Brad sat on an armchair, her in the seat and Brad on the side with his arm around her.

After a while, Gray took a deep breath and wiped his eyes. He asked how Pat was doing. "He slept through everything," Iris said.

Gray couldn't understand how that could be possible with the ambulance and noises and Muriel and Brad here and the weeping. He walked to the bedroom and looked down at Pat sleeping.

The little boy was completely still, his eyes shut as in a restful sleep. But he was too still. His legs were outstretched and his little arms at his side like a little soldier. Then Gray noticed tears rolled out of each eye, silently down the side of his face. Gray let him be.

Much later, Iris sat by herself in the darkened kitchen, sipping Jim's unfinished milkshake. She drank the last and looked at the glass for a long time, then went to the sink, poured Palmolive dish soap into it, washed it, dried it and placed it in the cupboard. She closed the door.

The black eastern sky started to glow into a dusty rose.

The day began cold and gray. Iris's courage left her as she stood outside the church where they had attended that special Christmas Mass so long ago. She faced it, her head on her chest, arms at her side, and cried like a little girl

Friends of the whole family attended the funeral and the gathering after the burial in Hardscrabble. The VMI alumni association sent flowers in a gold-rimmed bowl. The house was full of casseroles, roasts, breads, salads, and desserts Iris' friends had made.

Gray and Pam sat by themselves in the bedroom where Jim had died and looked down the crowded hallway to the crowded living room.

"I'm amazed," Pam said. "I've lived in Chicago apartments my whole life. I don't even know who my neighbors are! And these people, strangers to me bring food and flowers and hug me. It's incredible."

"That's Hardscrabble," Gray said.

Iris walked into the room.

"Gray, let me be alone with Pam for a while." She said. "And can you kind of watch to make sure we're not disturbed?" She was holding the baby Felicia, named after Bunny's sister, but handed her to Pam as she sat across from her.

Pam was guarded as Iris began.

"These last few months have been terrible for all of us. And now you're a widow like I was when I was your age. And now your baby doesn't have a father like Jim didn't have a father. You even had to live with your in-laws like I once did. But you'll learn that nothing, nothing is as important to you as a child. Not a husband or a home or a job or friends or anything. When Jim was suffering so badly I simply could not concentrate on anything. Maybe that was wrong...I don't know. Probably it was. I know it seems I ignored you. But it's a feeling that only a mother can experience."

The baby had a haze of strawberry hair. Pam looked up from her sleeping daughter.

"Iris, I couldn't understand a month ago. But today I can." She dared to wish she could have known Iris better in a different time, but they were both wounded now. They couldn't go back.

"Pam, you're young and will marry again. I know that must seem cold since Jim is just gone now. But in a way you are like me. We both knew our husbands so little when they died: it's not impossible to love again.

"If you do have more kids...well...just do the best you can and try not to blame yourself if things don't go the way you hoped. And remember each kid will be different. You raise them all the same way and feed them the same food, but they will still be different.

"I know Jim had a good life insurance policy, and you have social security, too. But could I have Jim's VMI ring? And I want Gray to have Jim's pistol and that ruby ring. He should have something of his brother's. I'll give the VMI ring to Felicia when she can understand, and Gray and Jim used that pistol when they went to target practice."

Pam would be much better off than Iris when her husband died, Iris thought.

Pam agreed and the mothers hugged. A few hours later, Pam and her baby would leave with her family for Chicago.

Gray, Pat and Iris walked in the yard, the grass crunchy from the cold. Suddenly, Iris knelt down next to the flowerbed, scooping at the snowdrifts. Pat and Gray looked at each other, baffled.

It was there: a sprout from a bulb. But it was too early for flowers.

"Why, this was the same time of the year that I came back from Washington. I felt then like half my world was over. I had two sons, no home and no husband. But I've got two sons again. And a home and a husband! And Jim left me a granddaughter!"

Gray had to tell her right then and there. "But Mom, I'm moving to Australia. I have to get out of here...from everything bad...I have to see things that Jim and my father never were able to. And Mom, you have a life of your own with Bill and Pat. It's only natural. This is your second family."

Iris was stunned. Then her features changed and smoothed.

Suddenly, she knew Jim was at peace. His pain was gone, and with it, hers. And Gray was a man.

"Yes! Go. Live."

Pat looked up at Gray. "But why go so far away?'

"Well, I'm 4-F so I don't have to go to Vietnam like other guys my age. I figure I should trade those years for something fun."

"But what did you get four F's in?"

Iris laughed and said, "Oh, it's complicated, honey. Say, why don't you go inside for a bit while I talk to Gray?" She watched him walk away, and then turned to Gray.

"Gray, something happened when Jim died." She gestured toward the lawn chairs and they sat facing each other. She knew Gray found it hard to stand too long.

"I thought I would go insane when Jim died. I had seen so much hurt and so much pain, that when the time came for Jim to...pass...I didn't think I could hold up. But when he looked at me, I seemed to read something all at once in his eyes. It was like he was trying to impart something in me that he was just beginning to understand. It was like he was saying, "It's a flow, Mom. We are all one. Everything is a part of a whole. We will all be restored and together. But he was too weak to form the words."

Iris continued, "And I felt this calm, like I was in the middle of a journey. I hope this doesn't sound funny, and I hope I'm explaining it right. Maybe my brain is just trying to keep me sane." She laughed slightly but Gray kept looking at her.

"I feel like Jim saw the other side, and with just one look he showed me. But it helped. It helped to heal me and make everything endurable."

"Well, I don't know," said Gray. "Some people think every living thing is related to each other, that we aren't individual men or women but we are all souls. A boy came from you, a girl came from Jim. Maybe we all come back together in the end. I guess it makes sense."

"I think," said Iris, "There's going to be some more hard times, but there are going to be many more good times. I think Jimmy wanted me to know that, that it's part of some great plan. I want to believe that.

"But I have to think, Gray, from what I know of illnesses, and I do know, I would want you or someone close to just 'pull the plug' if I get in a bad way."

Gray paused. "Mom, I don't know if I love you enough to do that."
Iris nodded, they stood, and Gray walked with his hand on Iris' shoulder.

Bill was in tears inside the basement bar. He was on his third bourbon, feeling no pain and getting everybody, like him, to roar with laughter with stories about Jim growing up.

"So there's Gray and Jimmy, hunting arrowheads in old man Kelly's field, stuck up to their knees in mud yelling 'Helllllp! Heeeellllp!'

"Iris and I were inside the house saying, 'What is that noise? Is that the dog howling like that? What's the matter with him?' "

"Hell, it took both of us and Ron next door to pull them out. Iris fell back and got her bottom stuck in the mud and then we had to pull HER out! Then we all had to hose the mud off each other in that freezing rain!

"We had to use two toothbrushes to get all the mud off of Gray's brace!"

He looked up as Iris and his boys listened and laughed with him.

"Come on upstairs. We've got an announcement!" she said. It felt so good to laugh again!

Gray knew the friends and family really needed to be cheered up and he tried to make his story fun as he got their attention.

"Well, a few months ago my girlfriend accepted a job at Sears in Chicago. Then my roommate got a job as a crime reporter for the Chicago Tribune." He paused. "She was talking about the benefits and the security and the retirement plans. And I said, 'Jan, we're 21! Who wants security? Who cares about retiring in 40 years? Let's go overseas for a couple years.' She just tuned out.

"Anyway, I had a job doing research on papers around Chicago and went over to the journalism building by myself on a Saturday morning. In a blizzard! I thought, *this will be the last blizzard of my life.* So there's a big book called 'Editor and Publisher' listing all the newspapers around the world. I wrote to The Daily Mirror in Sydney, Australia, and the editor named Rupert Murdoch said if I pay my own way down there they would hire me! For $54 a week."

He laughed. "How could I pass up $200 a month? I've taken out my immigration papers already.

"I told Jim right before he died."

Pam whispered to Iris, "Aaahh. The ship. That's what Jim meant."

The room was silent. Then Muriel spoke up, hesitatingly, "But Gray...what about your mother? Jim just died."

Gray already knew the answer but he let Iris speak.

"I love my boys and know they love me whether they are in heaven or at the dinner table or 10,000 miles away. I say 'have fun!' Life is too darn short!"

Just as the clapping started, Gray whispered, "12,000 miles, Mom."

The reception was breaking up. Ruth stopped to talk to Gray. They had dated several years before and it was one time Gray dared let himself love. Ruth was brainy in glasses and ravishing without them, and she had touched Gray.

It was on their fifth date that he had met her mother. She looked him up and down and said, "Ruth, is that the best you can do?"

It was the end of many things for Gray as he looked at Ruth's mother, then past her at the glass of Scotch on the table and the ashtray overflowing with butts. Then he remembered what his mother had said at the hospital many years ago about the black boy, George. Ruth and Gray broke up shortly after.

"So, Austria, how exciting," Ruth said. "Australia, yeah," Gray corrected.

"You are so lucky," she said.

"And you are so like your mother," Gray said, smiling, thinking perhaps he was lucky in one sense after all. "Tell me why you think getting this job had anything to do with luck."

When no response came he continued, "I heard you're marrying the guy at the Chevy dealership in town. Let's keep in touch."

Gray and Muriel had left the church earlier that day to clear away the wheelchair, the walker, and the stuff of illness from the bedroom, replace the rugs, and it was normal again.

Iris didn't ask what they did with it all.

That night Iris was saying goodnight to her sons in their twin beds.

She sat next to Pat. "Honey, I hope you don't feel I've ignored you these past few weeks. I had to take care of Jimmy."

Pat was indignant. "Gee, I knew that Mom. I'm not a little boy."

She smiled and brushed back his hair. "Oh, be my little boy for a little while longer."

"Well, okay. Just for a year."

Iris tilted her head back and laughed out loud.

She kissed him goodnight and went to Gray.

They both looked at the wall for a few moments.

Bill had put a backing on the jigsaw puzzle of the sailing ship, and then built a pine frame around it. He put a layer of shellac over the puzzle and stained the pine to match the dresser and hung it there. No one had asked him to do it; he just thought it would be a nice thing to do.

"I hope you won't be lonely in Sydney."

The lines from the movie 'Moulin Rouge' he had just seen flashed in his mind. The crippled Toulouse Lautrec was leaving the security of his family's country chateau to live in Paris.

"Mon cheri, I worry that you will be lonely in Paris," she said.

"Mais Moma, I will be lonely everywhere I go."

Gray smiled and said, "Well, if they don't like me I'll come back to Hardscrabble."

She stood up. "You won't be coming back to Hardscrabble." As she walked out of the bedroom she remembered her own words when she was about Gray's age as she was leaving on the train for Washington.

The pillow smacked into Pat's head just as Iris closed the door. "Nitey-nite, little boy," Gray teased.

Pat stood up in bed laughing and fired the pillow back. "Nitey-nite, big, ugly brother." The pillow missed Gray and landed on the dresser, scattering everything everywhere.

"Knock it off you two and go to sleep," Bill called out from the other bedroom.

Pat and Gray looked at each other in mock horror and pulled the blankets over their heads.

Iris slipped into bed and pulled Bill's heavy arm around her. "Maybe things will get back to normal."

Then she had to say it. "You sure took on a lot when you married me, Bill."

Bill was the son of a farmer, and uneducated beyond high school, but his words were eloquent.

"You and the boys gave my life meaning." His voice cracked. "You are a great lady."

In a flash Iris remembered the porter from the train who said that. Gray had said that once, too.

"And I did help you, didn't I?" Bill's voice cracked.

She was flushed with love and relief. They kissed for a very long time.

———⊗⊗⊗———

"Dear Gray," Iris wrote a few weeks later to Gray at school. "As luck would have it, Brad dated a woman when he was in Sydney when he was there during the war. She's married now and has three boys a little bit younger than you. Even though they hadn't been in contact for thirty years he wrote her and they're friends again.

"She insists you stay with them for a couple weeks till you get settled. They have a house right overlooking Bilgola Beach, about 15 miles north of Sydney."

And that was that. Iris felt more content, and Gray was happy. Since he was an immigrant he didn't like the idea of living in a hostel, job or no job.

He answered her back, and said, "Just for the heck of it I went to the gym where prospective employers look over candidates. I didn't tell them I was moving away. But I know by their attitude they just don't think a handicapped person would be the right image for the job. I remember what you told me of Roosevelt not wanting people to know. He was elected 3 times and he still knew people wouldn't approve of him because he wasn't normal. Things haven't changed."

Gray finished his classes, and audited a shorthand class, as shorthand was required for the position. He was the only boy amongst 35 girls so he had lots of advice. Iris thought it so remarkable that she had to learn shorthand when she left Hardscrabble, too.

———⊗⊗⊗———

There was happiness, yes, when Bill, Iris and Pat took Gray to O'Hare Airport for his two-week flight to Los Angeles, Hawaii, Tahiti and New Zealand, stopping in each place, and finally, Sydney. None of them had been on a plane before, and it was exciting, but sad for Iris.

Coming home, Pat spoke some of her thoughts. "Now I don't have any brothers."

In her efforts to cheer him up she cheered herself up. "Oh, but won't it be exciting to get letters from Gray and hear all about everything? He's stopping in Hawaii. I bet he sends us a postcard! I know, let's make a scrap board for all the cards. Maybe you can check the mail in a few days."

It worked. "Will he see a kangaroo when he gets to Sydney, you think?" He was sure they would be hopping around the airport.

Chapter 10

1972

Years had passed. At first Iris thought he would be back within a couple months, but a year passed, and then, two. Then, three. Gray loved the country and the people and would write regularly at least every other week. He wasn't "on the phone" there so there were no phone calls. Actually, Iris preferred letters so they could be kept and read. She thought about all those letters of Bunny's she had burnt, regretting doing it now, as Gray should have had them.

Things couldn't have been better at home. Pat had the attention of being an only child and still had a brother overseas he would write to. Bill worked for a large garage with more pay and less responsibility.

But Gray was Iris' only link now with her past life. She wanted to see him again soon. She wrote and asked him to come back for a visit.

Gray had a better idea. Why not get Muriel and Brad and have the four of them come there for a visit? It was impossible, and too complicated, and too much to coordinate. And they all agreed it was a fine idea.

By then Gray was working with Qantas Airways and could get a healthy discount on airfare. They couldn't afford not to go. Iris became a wonderful pain to her friends as she gave moment-by-moment accounts of the journey preparation. The climates were the opposite down there, you know, she said, hoping full well they didn't realize that so she could explain it. Passports, visas, someone to take care of Pat.

And this time it was their turn to go to O'Hare. Gray opened their world.

It was February, and late summer and stormy in Sydney. The red tile roofs from the plane looked gray. The gleaming white Opera House looked gray. The blue waters of the harbour looked gray.

Iris took it in stride, showing Gray the menu they had, the in-flight magazine, stories of the staff serving them real, free champagne when they found out they had a relative with Qantas.

Iris was wide-eyed from the moment she landed...people driving on the wrong side of the street...that strange English she could barely understand. Muriel commiserated. And Brad was glad to see there weren't soldiers everywhere as he remembered.

Every day after was blue, glorious and sunny. There were lunches on the beaches, harbour cruises and visits to the zoo and botanical gardens and a tour of the Opera House. A friend rented a Halverson cruiser and they hunted oysters on the twisting Hawkesbury River north of Sydney.

One day, Gray bought them lunch: delicious and greasy fish and chips and Chico Rolls and meat pies, all wrapped in The Daily Mirror newspaper that he had worked for.

They sat on the sand of Newport Beach, just down from Gray's apartment on Bardo Road.

Iris kept looking up at something.

"Mom, you act like you've never seen a palm tree before." He hoped she would remember.

"It's better than wallpaper, honey," she said.

The others smiled at their unshared secret.

One night, after friends had "shouted" his family at a beachside pub, Gray drove them back to their hotel. Iris had won $20 on the "poker" machines, slots in America.

Iris turned to Muriel, "Oh, weren't they all so nice? And Mrs. Tierney. I loved talking to her."

Muriel did not say anything, then, "You know, her accent was so strong I couldn't understand a word she said."

Immediately, Iris responded, "You know, I couldn't either!" Gray laughed so hard he had to pull off to the side of the road.

The evening before they left to return home, there was a dinner at a Bondi restaurant. They ate a white fish called John Dory. There were fat prawns the size of fingers, the carpet bag steak was delicious, but as it was stuffed with oysters, Iris decided to pass. She liked hunting them, but not eating them.

There were many, many bottles of wine. It was a dinner she would never forget.

Iris was able to get the gist of the conversation, despite the accents and the frivolity. Suddenly, she saw Gray stick his arm in the air and snap his fingers at the waiter who they learned was from Paris. "Garcon, encore du pain, si'l vous plait."

The waiter immediately brought a basket of bread rolls.

Gray. Speaking French. Iris was stunned. This was the little boy who was sometimes too shy to speak. She kept staring. Here he was, living on the other side of the world. Popular. Admired. Speaking French.

Gray happened to glance over at her, and he stared back, seeming to read her mind.

He raised his glass. She raised hers. It was a wonderful moment for Iris.

She looked around the table. She knew Gray preferred small groups of friends, but so many had wanted to host Gray's parents' last night that there were 12 people altogether.

It was a democratic group, Iris thought. Gray's choice of friends was always eclectic and he seemed to find something of interest in everyone he met.

There was a model, and a sheet metal worker; one couple ran their own green grocer business. Mrs. Tierney, a small insurance saleslady about Iris' age was there with her son. One friend was the president of a cigarette company, and years later would be president of Dunhill cigarettes in London and Atlanta. Iris noticed he smiled at Gray all through dinner.

Iris watched them eat, a knife in the right hand, the fork prongs down in their left. She turned to the man next to her, an office machine salesman, and smiled.

He was good looking, with clear skin, blue eyes and square jaw. He was heavier than Gray, and all muscle. He had been rowing for years. If this were Chicago he would be called "All American" so she supposed he should be called "All Australian."

Bob Tierney looked at her. "You have a hard time with our accents, don't you, Iris?"

"Well, thank you for saying that. If you speak slowly, I think I can understand," she whispered. She thought she had everybody fooled by her lack of understanding.

"Fair dinkum, Gray's my best mate. We've been dating the twins for a while." Iris looked over at Anne and at Maree.

They were from a turkey farm in Dubbo, but lived in Sydney. They both had stylish, flat blonde hair to their shoulders and light summer dresses that showed their slim figures very well, and a loose belt around the waist, which Iris guessed was Sydney fashion.

The girls wore too much eye make-up for Iris' taste, but this was the style. They were very sweet to Iris.

Iris turned to Anne, "Have you been dating Gray long?"

"Oh, just a fortnight, but we see each other every day. He's quite a catch, but I don't think anyone's going to catch him. He's very guarded with his affection."

Iris didn't know what to say but knew she was right.

"It must have been very difficult for you, Iris, a widow with two tykes, raising Gray in calipers."

Iris had never heard that word, and was startled at such a personal comment but knew from her eyes it was meant in the most understanding way.

"I...not really...I mean...well. Yes, it was," Iris finally stammered.

"Well, you did a bloody good job. We all love him," Anne said, squeezing her hand. "You are an inspiration to me. I want lots of kids."

Iris' heart choked her throat and she could only smile and look down at her plate, flushed.

Bob came to her rescue.

"Gray's had some wild parties at his beach house," Bob said, and then stopped. "I guess it's OK for me to say that?"

Iris laughed, and put him at ease. "There's nothing wrong with young people who have fun. Life is too short."

"Did Gray tell you I'll be rowing in the Olympics in Germany?" Bob asked. Without waiting for a reply he continued. He was talking faster but Iris caught most of it when she concentrated.

"Gray's inspired me to travel. I think I'll go to Canada on a working holiday after that. Maybe stay a couple years."

She remembered that meeting so often, especially a few years later when the call came.

The phone rang about 9 in the morning, and Iris answered it on the second ring. It was Gray. He had been working in San Francisco. She knew it must be important because it was only 7 there. He had difficulty speaking but she didn't interrupt.

"Mrs. Tierney called from the airport while I was at work. She had been visiting Bob in Vancouver and was on her way back to Sydney."

Iris could tell he had trouble breathing. Maybe he was crying.

"She said he had a nice girlfriend and they were living together, and that he liked his job and may stay another year.

"The flight is 17 hours. When she got to the Sydney airport her other son Brian was there. You met him when you were there. And lots of guys from the Drummoyne Rowing Club and their wives. They were all bawling.

"Bob's girlfriend's old boyfriend had broken into the apartment right after Mrs. Tierney left for the airport and chased them into the shower and shot and killed them both.

"Bob's friends knew it before the plane landed. Mrs. Tierney got off the plane ready to tell everyone how happy he was...and...His voice cut off.

Gray was crying for sure.

Iris wondered if there was anything crueler than being a mother. Bob had survived the Palestinian shooting at the Munich Olympics only to be killed in peaceful Canada. Life just wasn't fair. She would write a letter to Mrs. Tierney that night, from one mother who knew tragedy to another learning tragedy.

Three hours later the meal was finished after a Pavlova, a delicious concoc-
tion of meringue and cream and fruit. Iris scooted her chair back and took a
deep breath and exhaled.

"I am stuffed!" she exclaimed in a very broad Midwest American accent.
The restaurant stilled. Iris, puzzled, looked at Anne.

Anne leaned towards her smiling and whispered, "Iris, in Australia that
means you just made love!"

Iris' mouth dropped open as she stared at her dinner mates. Then she burst
out in the biggest laugh of her entire life as the table and the restaurant exploded
in good-natured hilarity and clinking glasses. Iris' favorite joke was when it was
on her.

That was the last time she would see Gray for many years. His work carried
him to the main capitols and his holidays carried him elsewhere. There were
postcards every month. Finally, while stationed in Paris he left the airlines to
become a writer. She guessed that had been his plan when he studied French.
He had a little apartment on the Left Bank, with the charming name, Passage
Dauphine. The offer was always open for Iris to visit, but it never worked out.
She was happy where she was.

They continued to exchange letters. Iris noted the subtle difference in his
phrasing and confidences. He questioned American politics and hypocrisy. He
seemed to analyze everything he had been taught. His friends were part of the
Paris riots in 1968 and Gray was fascinated by the stories of 'les flics.'

Iris had a bit of shopping to do, and in Hardscrabble that meant 25 per cent
shopping and 75 per cent visiting with friends along the way. This time, up
ahead, she saw Ruth's mother approaching. She hadn't heard anything about
her in a couple years since they had no friends in common and Iris was glad she
hadn't.

Iris remembered what Gray had told her, asking Ruth in front of him, "Is
that the best you can do?"

Although Gray had told her of that evening with Ruth and what her mother
had said to him, and he was very matter-of-fact about it, she knew it must have
hurt him.

Iris recalled standing at the kitchen window, lighting a cigarette and then putting her hand on the wall phone ready to call her and give her a piece of her mind. As she looked out the window at Gray holding Pat on his lap and laughing, she decided against it. Some people need to be popped, and for others even that doesn't do any good.

"Well, Iris," she said. "It's been so long. How are you and your family? Is Gray still at home?"

Iris caught the sarcasm and could barely smile, but that she did. "No, Gray is running a coffee shop and doing some writing. He only gets about a $100 a week but it comes with an apartment near the river."

"Oh, dear. A hundred dollars a week," she said, slowly, emphasizing every word. "In Hardscrabble?"

"No, in Paris."

"Oh, up near Peoria, on the Illinois River. A small town would be best, I suppose for someone like him."

Iris stirred and genuinely smiled. "No, dear, not that Paris. The capitol of France. The Seine. THAT Paris. His place is just down from where Madame Curie's husband was killed. He's seeing a beautiful French girl named Lydia. In fact, her mother works for the phone company, so Lydia and Gray and I just had a nice long talk for free! She sounds so sweet. She's a teacher, you know."

She paused for effect.

"But he plans on returning to his flat in Sydney, Australia later. He has it rented out. Such a nice view overlooking the Opera House."

No voice came out of the woman's open mouth.

Iris started again. "And Ruth. How is she?"

"Oh, she and the kids are living with me. She's separated."

Iris purposely took a long pause. "Oh, yes, that's right. The girls told me, but I guess I had forgotten. Tell her Gray and I said hello. And you can be sure I'll tell him I saw you. Bye."

Iris walked away. She was grinning.

Chapter 11

───────⊗⊗⊗───────

1998

G ray entered his flat back in Sydney and set his backpack on the marble table just as the phone rang. He answered it, glancing past the red geranium and kookaburras on the balcony and looked down at the busy harbour.

"G'day, this is Gray."

The voice was anxious. "Gray, where have you been? I've been trying for a week to get you." It was his brother, Pat.

"Some friends and I went to Tasmania. What is it? Is it Mom?"

"Yes. She fell more than a week ago. She broke her hip and hurt her head. Bad."

"She wants you. She says only you can help her now." Pat sounded bitter as he drew out each word.

"I'll head to Mascot now and call you from the airport. Meet me at O'Hare." Gray checked inside for his passport and traveler's checks. He then rang several friends.

Recognized as ex-Qantas, he was upgraded to First Class. Gray had hours and hours to think of his past with his mother.

Muriel was gone now, and Bill, and Brad, and many of her friends. His face showed his grief and the bleak future ahead. When he ordered a Bacardi and coke, the stewardess studied him and said, "I think I'll bring you a double."

"Ta," Gray replied.

Pat and Gray took care of the pleasantries after so many years apart. Pat looked much like Bill and even had his swagger when he walked. He slowed for Gray.

Pat had hired two ladies to take care of Iris when she was released from the hospital the day earlier. He had left his family and work in Chicago.

They entered Iris' tidy split-level apartment, as she sat there with the two heavy ladies with very warm smiles.

"Gray? Is that you?" Iris said. "What are you doing home from college?"

Everyone glanced at each other without moving their heads.

Gray and Iris kissed.

"I've come to take care of you, Mom. Got to help these nice ladies out." Gray nodded at the women.

Iris was Ida. She looked like a doll in her pink nightgown with ruffled collar. She now looked smaller, more vulnerable. Remote. Her eyes didn't seem to focus or grasp. Her leg was outstretched.

After Pat left for his home in Inverness, Gray studied her home. It struck him that this was the first home she had ever had by herself. No girlhood home, no D.C. roommates, no first family, no second family.

The apartment was clean and comfortable with many of the furnishings he had grown up with, exactly like Gray had expected. Above her desk were shelves with all the post cards and souvenirs he had sent...from Tokyo, Rio, Lake Baikal, Cape Town, Anchorage, Dublin, Moscow and other places. Many of the travel stories he wrote were posted on the wall. Gray leaned forward and re-read part of his article on the Trans-Siberian Railway.

The photo the White House had taken of him and President Clinton at the base of Air Force One was there. That was in Palm Springs. Iris was so proud of that. She had knocked on every apartment in the building to show it off when he sent it to her.

Not just of that, but that her prediction had come true. He did meet the president.

He came to learn that Iris' mind was often in another space, and Iris could only speak of present times, certainly nothing of yesterday, but sometimes of years past. Was it dementia, or Alzheimer's or the stroke or the anesthesia from the hip operation? It didn't matter. The result was what mattered.

The women worked in 10-hour shifts. They would take turns, arriving in mid-afternoon to prepare Iris, and then leave shortly after breakfast and bathing. One day, Gray sat alone with Iris as the caretaker prepared Iris' bath.

"Mom, the ladies said you aren't doing your leg exercises. You know you have to keep those muscles limber."

There was no reply, but Iris put her head down and stuck out her lower lip.

"I've been here a fortnight, and I think they're right."

Her brow furrowed. "You sound like Bob Tierney." Gray laughed.

"Mom, my home is in Australia now so I talk like he used to. You remember that. I took a year away so I could help you."

Her eyes troubled Gray. The clarity, maybe even the intelligence there was somehow clouded.

One evening as a caregiver and Iris watched television, Gray and a high school friend, Vince met at the local bar. They both ordered a Schlitz and grabbed a hard-boiled egg from the bar and sat in a booth.

"I don't know what to do, Vince." Gray began. "Sometimes Mom is so lucid, just like you and I remember her, and then she just goes into another space. That worries me more than her leg."

Vince didn't interrupt.

"Yesterday arvo...I mean afternoon...she said she wanted to go shopping, so we got her walker and went to Kroger's. I was pushing the basket and she would just grab a jar or can off the shelf and stand there and just study the ingredients. Vince, I lost my temper. I mean, why do you have to read the ingredients in a jar of pickles? I think I hurt her feelings when I said that. I was so sarcastic. But the worst part is..." Gray hesitated.

"When I would ride a bike my good leg would get so tired I knew I had to get off. I pretended that something was wrong with the seat or the spokes and would act like I was getting a twig or something out just so people wouldn't know I was resting.

"I think that's how Mom is. I think she just stops and tries to remember where she is and what she's doing there and doesn't want to appear feeble-minded or confused. We both had our pride. Then she gets going again."

"Well, Gray, maybe just fix what can be fixed," Vince said. "Get her walking again, and see what happens with her mind later."

"Yeah, good advice."

Just as Muriel and Iris had talked about Gray's health and then social events many years before, the discussion moved from Iris to the town and old times in high school.

Days and weeks rolled into each other, and Gray watched as his mother faded in front of his eyes. She would light a whole pack of matches just to see the flames leap in front of her. He watched her mix her mashed potatoes in with the car keys. There was no reason for optimism.

Pat would call from Chicago, asking about Iris, and the two talked of rest homes. They both knew Iris would rather be dead than a 'zombie' in a sterile clinic, but there were no options.

One day, the caretakers were at lunch, and Gray and Iris were alone. Iris had been quiet and strangely thoughtful. Often, the caregivers and Gray asked Iris what she was thinking when she got like this. All she would say was "things."

Earlier that day Iris had heard one of the girls ask the other if Iris would ever be 'normal.' Normal! How Gray must have hated it when people wondered out loud about him. She remembered every word Nurse Jeri had said long ago.

That one word, "things" nagged at Gray.

"Mom, when you have something on your mind you don't talk. And you're not talking now. What's the matter?"

Iris looked away and Gray knew she wouldn't confide. It was time to get back to business.

"OK, Mom. I'll get the walker and watch you walk back and forth. We have to get the bones to knit and exercise your muscles."

"I'll do that." She smiled. "But you have to tell me about the world out there I'm missing out on," Iris said.

"Deal." Gray smiled in return.

That was the routine now, day after day once the caretakers took their leave. Iris would walk back and forth; Gray would correct her posture, making her put more pressure on her legs and less on her arms. More using her calf muscles than relying on the wheels of the walker. Iris listened as Gray told her of the world she had envisioned for herself. Each day was a new city or country.

It was the Trans-Siberian railway and Lady Persia, and the nurse Alexandria he had traveled with. It was Dee and the Grand Hotel in Rhodesia. Michael, and hitching through Switzerland. His suspicions he was being followed near the insect zoo in Tokyo. The opera in Sydney, and the glowing ferries gliding across the black harbour. The apartment in Paris, and cobblestone echoes of footsteps at night. The glittering treasures of the Kremlin and Catherine the Great's golden carriage. Diving into the icy waters of Crete, and being tumbled about by the waters off Cape Town. The thundering waterfalls of Iguassu. The black market trade with a stranger in a Moscow toilet. Bad oysters in Dubrovnik. Each day was a different story and each day the same monotonous exercise.

Iris wasn't getting better; she was getting weaker. But she reveled in Gray's stories, proud in the excitement of her having dared him with world adventure if he would lose those braces. Maybe she had done something right, she thought.

Then the day came.

"Mom, the doctors said you have to start stair exercises. Let's start now while it's just the two of us."

Iris leaned back against the comfort of her sofa.

"No. It'll hurt."

"I have to hurt you to help you," Gray said. "Don't you want to get well?"

The words were identical to hers years ago. He pushed the walker towards her.

She touched her bathrobe pocket and then stood up, wobbly. It took almost five minutes for her to stand and walk toward the stairs where Gray was seated. He watched every move; wanting desperately to help her but making her do it alone.

He inched up the stairs as Iris pushed away the walker and reached the double-handed rails Pat had installed.

It took almost a minute for her to ascend each stair. Ten minutes later she reached the top where Gray sat, buried her face in her hands, and burst into tears of fatigue and pain and frustration.

"Why me, Gray? Why did this have to happen to me?" She removed her glasses and rubbed her eyes, then looked directly at him, remembering something.

As Gray looked in her eyes they both remembered that day so many years ago when Iris told him he was a brave boy.

"Mom, there's no reason for many things to have happened. It wasn't your fault what happened to me and it isn't your fault what happened to you.

Iris reached for his hand and said nothing. Her thumb traced his ruby ring.

"Mary and Lois will be so proud of you, Mom. That was hard work, I know."

She looked at him again, her eyes murky, like moonstone.

"They're your caretakers, Mom. You remember."

"No."

Iris began, "The day your father died," and Gray was taken aback at the change in subject and the fact that Iris could not remember from this morning but wanted to talk about something that happened so many years ago.

"I was washing dishes and saw the jeep with Bunny and your grandfather coming in the distance, and then go down a hill. But it didn't come up. I waited, and just as I was about to check on them your grandfather walked up rubbing one hand. He said he had dislocated a finger and I rubbed it and he said that helped.

"Finally he said, 'Bunny fainted,' so I ran down the hill and Bunny was there at the steering wheel and was unconscious. But there was a bruise on the side of his mouth.

"Jim drove the jeep back while I sat in the back holding Bunny's head. When we carried him into the house I took off his new boots, and he just didn't wake up. Jim kept saying, 'He's dead, he's dead.'

"But your grandfather wasn't in shock or anything, it's like he was mad at him for dying. The doctor said it was cerebral hemorrhage, but...

"I left the day of the funeral. If something did happen between them I didn't want to know it. Granddad was so mad at me taking Jimmy...I mean, and you, of course, away he didn't give me a cent."

Iris paused, choosing her words.

"Our little town doctor...if he knew anything...didn't say anything. After all...your grandparents were prominent in that town. It was just a little town... kind of like Hardscrabble. The same kind of doctor.

"There was no reason to report it. What was done was done."

She stared into his eyes.

The real death of his father staggered Gray, yet at the same time seemed wholly plausible. And something he could not think about now. It had to be put on hold. Iris was building up to something.

Gray knew there was something in the meaning of her words but couldn't catch it.

"Yes, you were a brave boy, and I know you're a brave man now. I remember so often I'd be in the basement putting the wet clothes in the basket and how tired I got going up and down the stairs on washing day. But I looked at you going up those same steps so slowly and carefully, and well...it gave me my strength. Now I want you to be strong for me, Gray. I'm not going to get any better. I can't even remember things that happened 10 minutes ago. Pretty soon I won't be able to even...you know...take care of myself. That's not the way I want to live and not the way I want to die. I won't go into a nursing home. Don't think I don't know what you and Pat have been discussing. I can't live like this... with no dignity.

"A long time ago I told Muriel how much I envied Jackie Kennedy when she got married. I was sure she was going to have a great life and I was really kind of jealous. And look what happened to her. But I remember her son was with her when she died and he said, 'She was surrounded by her family, and did it in her own way and on her own terms.'

"I want to do it in my own way and on my own terms."

She reached into her pocket and showed Gray the pills.

"The doctor, when he gave me these pills, looked me straight in the eyes. He said, 'Now, Iris, make sure you don't take more than four at one time. They can be very dangerous.'

"Gray, I knew what he was saying."

"But...but what about God?" Gray offered.

Iris glanced across the room at Jim's VMI graduation picture. "Oh, I think He owes me a couple," she said.

They paused again. There was not a sound in the house except for the ticking of the clock and the gas blower turning on as the afternoon waned.

"You have to be strong for me," she said.

"Oh, you were the weak one we all worried about. When you were in the hospital one time little Jimmy and your dad and I joined hands and swore we would protect you the rest of your life. Now you will outlive all of us.

"I wouldn't want a sudden death like your father. But I don't want a lingering, painful death like Jim had. But I just can't be wheeled and carried around. Not at my age. What's the point? And I want to leave you and Pat a little something. I don't want that money swallowed up in some corporation."

The old lady was gone. Gray saw only the clear face and bright eyes and bouncing hair of his young mother.

"When do you want it to...happen, Mom?"

"I want to call Pat and his family just to talk. But this will be our secret. I can... what's the expression...over-medicate myself. I've been saving up my pain pills all this time. The girls don't know. But I want you near me to say goodbye. I can do it alone, but I want you to be there for me when I need you."

"*Dignity had been her gift to me,*" Gray thought. "*What could be more important than helping her? Should morality and law overshadow suffering? After all, France allows help, but America insists that the dying be assisted till they are broke and dead. Probably a home for one month would equal all the years of my polio treatment through the March of Dimes.*"

Iris closed her eyes while Gray thought.

Gray remembered their conversation after Jim's funeral so many years before.

"OK, Mom. I do love you enough. You decide for sure tonight. Then, tomorrow after the girls leave...near the south window. You can see outside. The sky will be clear. The snow's gone...it's warm...I can open the window...the sun will be on you and you can see the trees and the flowers."

"No, Gray," Iris corrected. "It's too early for flowers.

THE END

AFTERWORD

Iris Ohlinger Sipolski Mondy died 50 years to the day Gray was diagnosed with polio.

"Polio" is Latin for Gray.

"The Radium Girls" topic has many historical references, and most recently was the subject of a musical, "Shining Lives."

ABOUT THE AUTHOR

Kurt Sipolski was raised in Streator, Illinois, originally called Hardscrabble. He studied journalism at Northern Illinois University in DeKalb, and graduated in 1968.

Immediately after graduation, he was hired by Rupert Murdoch to work as a reporter on his Cumberland Newspaper chain in Parramatta, New South Wales, outside Sydney.

However, when acquaintances admired his NIU class ring, he contacted the manufacturer in Texas, and Kurt introduced class rings to Australia and became the marketing coordinator, working for Angus & Coote jewellers.

He became very familiar with Australian opals.

Kurt worked in Paris at International House, a private language school, and traveled in Europe backpacking before moving back to Sydney, and began working with Ansett Airlines, then Qantas Airways until he was transferred to San Francisco.

There he founded and published San Francisco Gentry magazine, which he sold to move to Palm Desert, California.

He has worked as an "extra" in several productions, including "Bugsy" and "Ruby," and now writes freelance and likes to landscape. "Rich men have therapists. Poor men have gardens," is his mantra.

Kurt was asked to read from "Flowers" at a Wounded Warriors seminar in Maine, and also at various Rotary Clubs near Palm Springs. The original memoir was published on the Rotary online site.

And yes, he did meet President Clinton in Palm Springs.

Most recently, Kurt was asked to share this novella at a writer's seminar in Paris. He retraced his steps from decades before, only this time on crutches. The photo on the back cover was taken in the Marais district.

He has signed an option for screen rights of "Too Early for Flowers."

.

Made in the USA
San Bernardino, CA
28 August 2016